"Hot damn!"

Sherry opened one eye and saw a girl of about twelve, dressed in jeans and a red plaid shirt, standing just inside the doorway.

"Hot damn," the girl repeated, smiling as if it were Christmas morning and she'd found Santa sitting under the tree waiting for her.

"What time is it?" Sherry rubbed her eyes and groaned. It felt as if she'd arrived at the ranch house and fallen asleep only minutes ago.

"Eight-thirty. Where's Dad?"

"Um...you're Heather?"

"So he mentioned me, did he?" the girl asked gleefully. She walked into the room and leapt onto the mattress, making it bounce.

"I think you have the wrong impression of what's going on here," Sherry felt obliged to tell her.

"You're in my dad's bed, aren't you? That tells me everything I need to know!"

Dear Reader,

I confess, I don't own a pair of cowboy boots, a hunting rifle, a pickup truck or a thousand-acre ranch. Oil, to those of us up north, is something you stir-fry with. But I've been to Texas—twice—and I loved it both times. The people are wonderful and I was able to pick up the language without much difficulty. I learned there is something known as a real Texan. He's the guy with the boots, the pickup truck and a buckle the size of a chastity belt.

When my editor asked me to contribute to the BACK TO THE RANCH series, I knew immediately where I wanted to set my story. Where else but Texas? Just imagine a feisty gal from the north running into one of those real Texan men! Sounds like fun already, doesn't it?

Some of you might remember Sherry Waterman from *Valerie,* the first book of the ORCHARD VALLEY trilogy. I've received a number of requests to write a book for Sherry, and this seemed the perfect opportunity. My feisty heroine popped up eager and ready. Sherry's hero is a rancher by the name of Cody Bailman. Naturally he's a real Texan male! He's also got a matchmaking daughter—and as they say, the rest is history.

I hope you enjoy this story. I promise you a few chuckles along the way as this Texas cowboy meets his match. And I'd love to hear from you; you can reach me at P.O. Box 1458, Port Orchard, Washington 98366.

Sincerely,

Debbie Macomber

LONE STAR LOVIN'
Debbie Macomber

Harlequin Books

TORONTO • NEW YORK • LONDON
AMSTERDAM • PARIS • SYDNEY • HAMBURG
STOCKHOLM • ATHENS • TOKYO • MILAN
MADRID • WARSAW • BUDAPEST • AUCKLAND

ISBN 0-373-03271-4

Harlequin Romance first edition July 1993

LONE STAR LOVIN'

CHAPTER ONE

"YOU'RE A LONG WAY from Orchard Valley," Sherry Waterman muttered to herself as she stepped out of her GEO Storm and onto the main street of Pepper, Texas. Heat shimmered up from the black asphalt.

Drawing a deep breath, she glanced around with an appraising eye at this town, which was to be her new home. Pepper resembled any number of small mid-Texas towns she'd driven through in the past twenty-four hours.

The sun was pounding down with a vengeance, and Sherry wiped her brow with her forearm, looking for someplace to buy a cold drink. She was a couple of weeks early; she'd actually planned it this way, hoping to get a feel for Pepper and the surrounding ranch community before she took over her assignment. In an hour or so she would drive on to Houston, where she'd visit her friend Norah Cassidy for a couple of weeks, then double back to Pepper. Although it was considerably out of her way, she was curious about this town—and the job she'd accepted as a physician's assistant, sight unseen, through a medical-employment agency.

Her small car didn't have air-conditioning, and she'd rolled down both windows in an effort to create a cooling cross-draft. It had worked well enough, but along with the breeze had come a fine layer of dust, and a throat as dry as the sun-baked Texas street.

Clutching her purse and a folded state map, she headed for the Yellow Rose café directly opposite. A red neon sign in the window promised home cooking.

After glancing both ways, she jogged across the street and hurried into the, thankfully, air-conditioned café. The counter was crowded with an array of cowboy types, so she seated herself by the window and reached for the menu tucked behind the napkin canister.

A waitress wearing a pink gingham uniform with a matching ruffle fixed in her hair strolled casually toward Sherry's table. "You're new around these parts, aren't you?" she asked by way of greeting.

"Yes," Sherry answered noncommittally, looking up from the menu. "I'll have an iced tea with extra lemon and a cheeseburger, without the fries." No need to clog her heart arteries with extra fat. The meat and cheese were bad enough.

"Iced tea and a cheeseburger," the waitress repeated. "You wanna try our lemon meringue pie? It's the best this side of Abilene."

"Oh, sure, why not?" Sherry said, giving up the cholesterol battle without a fight. The waitress left and returned almost immediately with the iced tea. Sherry drank long and gratefully, then spread the map across the table and charted her progress. With luck, she should be able to reach Houston by midafternoon the following day. Right on schedule. Her friend, Norah Cassidy, wasn't expecting her before Wednesday, so Sherry could make a leisurely drive of it—though she'd enjoy the drive a whole lot more if it wasn't so hellishly hot.

The waitress brought Sherry's cheeseburger on a thick, old-fashioned ceramic plate. A mound of onion and tomato slices, plus lettuce and pickles, were neatly arranged next to the open burger.

"Don't see too many strangers coming this way," the waitress commented, plopping down containers of mustard and ketchup. "Most folks stick to the freeway."

"I prefer driving the back roads," Sherry said, popping a pickle slice into her mouth.

"You headed for San Antonio?"

"Houston. I'm a physician's assistant and—"

"I don't suppose you're looking for a job?"

Sherry smiled to herself. "Not exactly. I already have one." She didn't add that the job was right here in Pepper.

"Oh." The eager grin faded. "The town council's been advertising with one of those employment agencies for over a year."

Apparently the waitress hadn't heard that they'd hired someone. "I'm also a nurse and a midwife," Sherry added, although she wasn't sure why she felt obliged to list her credentials for the woman. The physician's assistant part was a recent qualification.

The waitress nodded. "I hear lots of women prefer to have their babies at home these days. Most everyone around Pepper comes to the hospital, though."

"You have a hospital here?" This was welcome news. The town didn't look large enough to support more than a café, a couple of taverns and a jail.

"Actually it's a clinic. But Doc's made sure we've got the best emergency-room facilities within two hundred miles. Last year one of the high-school boys lost an arm, and Doc was able to save the arm *and* the kid. Wouldn't have been able to do it without all that fancy equipment. We're right proud of that clinic."

"You should be." Sherry gazed longingly at her lunch. If the waitress didn't stop chattering, it was going to get cold.

"You have family in Houston?"

Sherry added the rest of her condiments, folded the cheeseburger closed and raised it toward her mouth as a less-than-subtle hint. "No, just a good friend."

The woman's eyes brightened. "I see." She left and returned less than a moment later, a tall, potbellied older man in tow.

"Howdy," he said with a lazy drawl. "Welcome to Texas."

Sherry finished chewing her first bite. "Thank you. It's a wonderful state."

"What part of the country you from?"

Sherry's gaze lingered on her burger. "Oregon. A little town called Orchard Valley."

"I hear it's real pretty up there in Or-ee-gon."

"It's beautiful," Sherry agreed, dropping her gaze to her plate. If she was lucky, this cowpoke would get the message and leave her to her lunch.

"'Course living in Texas has a lot of advantages."

"That's what I understand."

"Suppose I should introduce myself," he said, holding out his hand. "Name's Dan Bowie. I'm Pepper's duly elected mayor."

"Pleased to meet you." Sherry wiped the mustard from her fingertips and extended her hand. He shook it, his eyes gleaming, then without waiting for an invitation, pulled out the chair opposite her and made himself comfortable.

"Little Donna Jo here was telling me you're a physician's assistant."

"That's true."

"She also said you already have a job."

"That's true too, but—"

"It just so happens that Pepper badly needs a qualified physician's assistant. Now, we've finally hired one, but she's not due to get here for a coupla weeks yet. So-o-o..."

Sherry abruptly decided to discontinue her charade. "Well, she's here. It's me." She smiled brightly. "I'm early, I know, but—"

"Well, I'll be! This is great, just great. I wish you'd said something sooner. We'd've thrown a welcome party if we'd known, isn't that right, Donna Jo?"

"Actually I was on my way to Houston to visit a friend, but curiosity got the better of me," Sherry explained. "I thought I'd drive through town and get a look at Pepper."

"Well, what do you think?" He pushed back his Stetson and favored her with a wide smile. "You can stay for a little while, can't you?" he asked. "Now you finish your lunch," he said as Donna Jo set a towering piece of lemon meringue pie in front of Sherry and replenished her iced tea. "Your meal's on us," he announced grandly. "Send the tab to my office, Donna Jo."

"Thank you, but—"

"Soon as you're done, Miz..."

"Waterman. Sherry Waterman."

"Soon as you're done eating, I aim to show you around town. We'll mosey by the clinic, too. I want Doc Lindsey to meet you."

"Well...I suppose." Sherry hoped she didn't sound ungracious. She finished her meal quickly and in silence, acutely conscious of Mayor Bowie's rapt and unwavering gaze.

The second she put her fork down, he took hold of her elbow and lifted her from the chair. He'd obviously regained his voice, because he was talking enthusiastically as he guided her out the café door.

"Pepper's a sweet little town. Got its name from Jim Pepper. Don't suppose you ever heard of him up there in Or-ee-gon. He died at the Alamo, and our forefathers didn't want the world to forget what a fine man he was, so they up and named the town after him. What most folks don't know is that he was darn near blind. He couldn't have shot one of Santa Ana's men if his life depended on it, which unfortunately it did."

"I'm sure his family was proud."

They strolled down the road and turned left onto a friendly-looking, tree-lined street. Sherry noticed a huge old white house with a wide porch and dark green shutters and guessed it must be the clinic.

"Doc Lindsey's going to be mighty glad to meet you," the mayor was saying as he held open the gate of the white picket fence. "He's been waiting a good long while for this. Yes, indeed. A good long while."

"I'm looking forward to meeting him, too," Sherry said politely. And it was true. She'd spent the better part of two years going to school part-time in order to train for this job. She was looking forward to beginning her new responsibilities. But not quite yet. She did want to visit Norah first.

She preceded the mayor up the porch steps to the screen door. He opened it for her, and led her inside, walking past a middle-aged receptionist, who called out a cordial greeting.

"Doc's in, isn't he?" Dan asked over his shoulder, without stopping to hear the reply.

Apparently, whether or not Doc was with a patient was no concern to Pepper's duly elected mayor. Guiding her by the elbow, he knocked loudly on a polished oak door and let himself in.

An older white-haired man was sitting in a comfortable-looking office chair, his feet propped on the corner of a scarred desk. His mouth was wide open, his head had fallen back. A strangled sound came from his throat, and it took Sherry a moment to realize he was snoring.

"Doc," Dan said loudly. "I brought someone for you to meet." When the old man didn't respond, Dan said it again, only louder.

"I think we should let him sleep," Sherry whispered.

"Nonsense. He'll be madder'n blazes if he misses meeting you."

Whereas the shouting hadn't disrupted Don Lindsey's nap, Sherry's soft voice did. He dropped his feet and straightened, blinking at Sherry as if she were an apparition.

"Who in tarnation are you?"

"Sherry Waterman," she said. "Mayor Bowie wanted us to meet."

"What ails you?"

"I'm in perfect health."

"She's that gal we hired from Or-ee-gon."

"Why in heaven's name didn't you say so sooner?" Doc Lindsey boomed, vaulting to his feet with the energy of a man twenty years younger. "About time you got here."

"I'm afraid there's been some misunderstanding...." Sherry began, but neither man was listening. Doc slapped the mayor across the back, reached behind the door for his fishing pole and announced he'd be back at the end of the week.

He hesitated on his way out of the office. "Ellie Johnson's baby is due anytime now, but you won't have a problem with that. More'n likely I'll be back long before she goes into labor. She was two weeks late with her first one."

"Don't you worry," the mayor said, following Doc out the door. "I heard Sherry tell Donna Jo she's a midwife too."

Doc shook hands with the mayor, and chortled happily. "You outdid yourself this time, Danny-boy. See you in a week."

"Dr. Lindsey!" Sherry cried, chasing after him. He was already outside and on the sidewalk. "I'm not staying! I'm on my way to Houston to meet a friend." She scrambled down the steps so fast she nearly stumbled.

Apparently Doc didn't hear her. The mayor seemed to have developed a hearing problem, too.

Doc tossed his fishing pole into the bed of his truck and climbed into the front seat.

"I can't stay!" she shouted. "I'm not scheduled to start work for another two weeks. I've made other plans!"

"Seems to me you're here now," Doc said. "Might as well start. Good to have you on the team. I'll see you..." The roar of the engine drowned out his last words.

Sherry stood on the lawn, her heart pounding as she watched him drive away. Frowning in frustration, she knotted her fists at her sides. Neither man had taken the trouble to listen to her; they just assumed she would willingly forgo her plans. But darn it, she wasn't going to be railroaded by some hick mayor and a doctor who obviously spent more time sleeping and fishing than practicing medicine.

"I can't stay," she announced, annoyed as much with herself as she was with the mayor for the mess she was in. This was what she got for being so curious.

"But you can't leave now," Mayor Bowie insisted. "Doc won't be back for a week. Besides, he's never been real good with time—a week could turn out to be ten days or more."

She pushed a stray lock of shiny brown hair off her forehead, and her blue eyes blazed. "That's unfortunate, because I'm meeting my friend in Houston and I can't be late." That wasn't entirely true but she didn't intend to start work until the agreed date. On top of that, she couldn't shake the feeling that there was something not quite right about the situation here in Pepper. Something was going on.

"If you could only stay the week, we'd all be mighty grateful," the mayor was saying.

"I'm sorry but no," Sherry stated emphatically, heading back down the street toward her car.

The mayor dogged her heels. "I'm sure your friend wouldn't mind. Why don't you phone and ask her? The city will pay for the call."

Great, Sherry thought, there were even perks. "No thanks," she said firmly.

The mayor continued to plead. "I feel right bad about this," he said. "But a week, why, only seven days, and Doc hasn't had time off like this in months."

Sherry kept walking, refusing to allow him to work on her sympathies. He seemed to have forgotten about the possibility of Doc's absence lasting as long as ten days, too.

"You have to understand," he went on, "that with Doc away there isn't anyone within miles for medical emergencies."

Sherry stopped and turned to glare at him. "It's unfortunate that the pair of you didn't think of that sooner. I told you when you introduced yourself that I was on my way to Houston. My contract doesn't start for two weeks."

"I know." He removed his hat and looked at her imploringly. "Surely a week isn't too much to ask."

"Excuse me, miss." A stocky police officer dressed in a tan uniform had come out of the café and moseyed over to her. The town sheriff, she decided. He was chewing on a toothpick and his thumbs were tucked in his belt buckle, which hung low under his protruding belly. "I don't suppose you happen to own that cute little GEO Storm, just there, do you?" He pointed at her car, about twenty feet away.

"As a matter of fact, I do."

His nod was slow and deliberate. The toothpick was smoothly transferred to the other side of his mouth. "I was afraid of that. As best I can tell, it's parked illegally."

"It most certainly is not," Sherry protested as the three of them reached the GEO. The slot was clearly marked and she had pulled in between two other vehicles.

"See how your left rear tire is over the yellow line?" the sheriff asked, pointing.

"I suppose that carries a heavy fine?" Good grief, she thought. Before long some cowpoke was going to suggest they get a rope and hang her from the nearest tree. In which case she was okay, since she hadn't seen anything but brush for the last hundred miles.

"There isn't a fine for illegally parking your car," he said, grinning lazily. "But jaywalking carries a hefty one, and I saw you cross that street with my very own eyes."

"There wasn't a crosswalk," she protested.

"Sure there is," he said, still grinning. "It's down the street a bit, but it's there. I painted it myself no more'n ten years ago."

"You're going to fine me, then," she said reaching into her bag for her wallet. "Great. I'll pay you and be done with it." She was going to head straight for the freeway, and when she reached Houston, she would reconsider this job offer.

"There isn't any fine."

"But you just said there was!" Actually, Sherry was greatly relieved. Her cash was running low and she doubted that the sheriff would accept a check.

"No fine, but the jail term—"

"Jail term!" she exploded.

"Now, Billy Bob," the mayor said, placing himself between the two of them, "you don't really intend to put our doc's helper in jail, do you?"

Billy Bob rubbed his hand across the underside of his jaw as if needing to contemplate such a monumental decision.

"You'd give Pepper a bad name," the mayor continued, "and we wouldn't want that, would we?"

"You staying in Pepper, miss?" the officer asked.

Sherry's gaze connected with Mayor Bowie's. "It appears I don't have much choice, do I?"

The minute she had access to a phone, Sherry vowed, she was going to call her friend's husband, Rowdy Cassidy. Rowdy, the owner of one of the largest computer software companies in the world, had a large legal staff at his fingertips. He'd be able to pull a few strings for her. By the end of the day, these folks in Pepper would be facing so many lawsuits, they'd throw a parade when she left town.

"I'll walk you back on over to the clinic," the mayor said, smiling as though he hadn't a care in the world. "I'm sure Mrs. Colson'll be happy to give you a tour of the place."

Sherry ground her teeth and bit back a tart reply. Until she had the legal clout she needed, there was no use in voicing any more protests.

Instead, Billy Bob himself escorted her down the street and around the corner to the clinic. The middle-aged receptionist introduced herself as Mrs. Colson and greeted Sherry with a warm smile. "I'm so pleased you decided to stay."

"You make her welcome now," the sheriff instructed.

"You know I will," Mrs. Colson told him, standing and coming around the short counter. "There's no need for you to stay," she told Billy Bob and, taking him by the elbow, escorted him out the door. She turned to Sherry. "Billy Bob can outstare a polecat, but beneath that tough hide of his, he's as gentle as a baby."

Sherry bit back a retort as the receptionist went on to extol the sheriff's virtues.

"One of those multitalented folks you read so much about. Not only does he uphold the law around these parts, but he makes the best barbecue sauce in the state. Just wait till you taste it. Everyone thinks he should bottle and sell it, but I doubt he will."

"How unfortunate," was the best Sherry could manage.

Her mood didn't improve as Mrs. Colson gave her the grand tour. Despite her frame of mind, Sherry was impressed with the clinic's modern equipment and pleased with the small apartment at one end of the building that would serve as her living quarters.

"Doc's sure glad to get away for a few days," Mrs. Colson said amicably, ignoring Sherry's sour mood. "I can't even remember the last time he had more than a day to himself. He talks about fishing all the time—gets a pile of those magazines and catalogs. In the twenty years I've known him, I don't believe I've seen him livelier than he was today after you arrived. Guess he was thinking he'd best skedaddle before you changed your mind. I'm sure glad you didn't."

Sherry's answering smile was weak. Between Dan Bowie, Doc Lindsey and Billy Bob, she'd been completely hog-tied.

"So Dr. Lindsey has been practicing in Pepper for twenty years?" She wondered if, like her, he'd innocently driven into town and been snared. This could be something straight out of "The Twilight Zone."

"Thirty years, in fact, maybe more. Most folks think of him as a saint."

Some saint. Sherry thought. With little more than a nod of his head, he'd abandoned Pepper and her.

Mrs. Colson led her to Doc's office. "Now make yourself at home. Do you want a cup of coffee?"

"No, thanks," Sherry answered, walking over to the desk. The telephone caught her eye. As soon as she had a minute alone, she would call Houston.

But the moment Mrs. Colson left there was a knock at the office door. Sherry groaned. She hadn't even had time to sit down.

"Come in," she called, thinking it must be the receptionist.

In walked a tall, rawboned cowboy with skin tanned the color of a new penny. He wore jeans, a checkered shirt and a pair of scarred boots. A Stetson hat hooded his dark eyes, and somehow, with the red bandana around his neck, he looked both rough and dangerous.

"You're not Doc Lindsey," he said accusingly.

"No," she agreed tartly, "I'm not."

"Oh, good," Mrs. Colson said, following him into the room. "I see your one-o'clock appointment is here."

"*My* one o'clock appointment?"

"Where's Doc?" the cowboy demanded.

"He's gone fishing. Now you sit down," Mrs. Colson directed in steel tones. "You're Miz Waterman's first patient, and I don't want her getting a bad impression about the folks in Pepper."

"I ain't talkin' to no woman about Heather."

"Why not? A woman would be far more understanding than Doc."

Personally, Sherry agreed with the cowboy.

"Don't you argue with me, Cody Bailman," Mrs. Colson said, arms akimbo. "I'll have your hide if you make trouble for Miz Waterman. She's a real sweetheart."

Cody shifted his hat farther back on his head and scratched his brow. "It ain't gonna work."

"That's right enough. It ain't gonna work unless you try." The receptionist took Cody by the elbow and marched him to the chair on the other side of the desk. "Now sit. You, too, Sherry." Neither of them bothered to comply, but that didn't disturb the receptionist. "Cody's here to talk about his daughter. She's twelve and giving him plenty of grief, and he comes for advice because...well, because his wife died about ten years back and he's having a few problems understanding what's happening to Heather now that she's becoming a young woman."

"Which means I'm not talkin' to some stranger about my personal affairs," Cody said.

"It'll do you good to get everything out," Mrs. Colson assured him. "Now sit down. Sherry, you sit, too. If you stand, it'll make Cody nervous."

Sherry sat. "What am I supposed to do?" she whispered.

"Listen," the older women instructed. "That's all Doc ever does. It seems to help."

Doc Lindsey apparently served as Pepper's psychologist, too. Sherry had received some training along those lines, but certainly not enough to qualify as a counselor.

"I'm not talkin' to a woman," Cody said.

"Did you ever consider that's the reason you're having so many problems with Heather?" Mrs. Colson pointed out, then stalked over to the door. As she reached for the knob, her narrowed gaze moved from Cody to Sherry, and her tight features relaxed into a reassuring smile. "You let me know if Cody gives you any problems, but I doubt he will. He's a dear once you get to know him." She dropped her voice. "What Heather really needs is a mother, and to my way of thinking, Cody should remarry."

"You volunteering for the job, Martha?" Cody said.

Mrs. Colson's cheeks pinkened. "I'm old enough to be your mother, and you darn well know it." With that she left the room, closing the door behind her.

Cody laughed and to Sherry's surprise sat down in the chair across from her, took off his hat and relaxed. As he rested one ankle on top of his knee and stared at Sherry, the humor drained out of his face.

She wasn't sure what she should do. If she hadn't felt so intimidated by this dark-haired cowboy, she'd have sent him on his way.

"You married?" He asked suddenly.

Her mouth dropped open. When she finally managed to speak, her words stumbled over one another.

"No, I'm not, I . . . that is . . ." She knew she sounded breathless and inane.

"Don't look so worried. I wasn't expecting you to volunteer as my wife."

"I realize that," she said with as much dignity as she could muster. Unfortunately it wasn't much.

"Then how are you supposed to know about kids?"

"I have two younger brothers and a sister," she said, wondering why she thought she had to defend herself. By all that was right, she *should* be sending him on his way. She sighed. The more this day progressed, the more convinced she was that she'd somehow stepped out of time. The man sitting across from her might have come from another century.

"So you know about girls?"

"I was one not so long ago myself," she said wryly. Resigning herself to the situation, she asked, "Why don't you tell me something about Heather and I'll see if I can help?"

Cody seemed to need time to think over her suggestion. "Well, first off, Heather's doing things behind my back."

"What sort of things?"

"Wearing makeup and the like. The other night I went in to check up on her and I swear she had on so much silver eye shadow her lids glowed in the dark."

Sherry swallowed her impulse to laugh.

"No more'n about six months ago," he continued, clearly confused by what was happening with his daughter, "Heather was showing signs of being one of the best cowhands I'd ever seen, but now she doesn't want to have anything to do with ranching. Besides that, she's getting bigger on top."

"Have you bought her a bra?"

He flushed slightly beneath his tan. "I didn't have to—she bought her own. Ordered it right out of the catalog before I even knew what she'd done. From what I can see, she didn't have a clue about what she was doing, because the one they sent was five sizes too big. Rather than admit she didn't know about such things, she's wearing it and as best I can tell stuffing it with something. Heaven only knows what."

"My guess is tissue." That had worked for Sherry when she was a teenager!

Cody's dark eyes narrowed in concentration. "Could be. I asked her about it, and she nearly bit my head off."

Mrs. Colson was right, the poor girl did need a mother.

"Has Heather got a boyfriend?" Maybe Cody was jealous of some boy. It sounded like a good theory anyway.

Cody frowned. "Ever since she's been wearing this bra, she'd got a whole passel of boys hanging around. The thing is, she doesn't like all this attention. You have to understand that until recently Heather was a tomboy."

"Heather's growing up, Cody," Sherry told him softly. She leaned back and crossed her arms. "She doesn't understand what's happening to her body. My guess is she's frightened by the changes. Trust me, she isn't any happier about the things that are taking place than you are. Give her a little time and a little space, and you'll be surprised by how well she adjusts."

Cody eyed her as if he wasn't sure he should believe her.

"Does she have any close friends?" she asked.

"Wally and Clem, but she doesn't seem to be getting along with them as well as she used to."

"What about girlfriends?"

"She has a couple, but they live here in town and we're twenty miles away. What she really needs is to talk to someone—you know, a woman, someone older than thirteen, who knows a bit more about things like bras and other girl stuff. And then there was this business with the 4-H—all of a sudden my daughter wants to run my life."

"The 4-H? Your life?"

"Never mind," he said, groaning heavily.

"Would you like me to try talking to her?" Sherry offered. "I...I don't know if I'd be able to accomplish anything, but I'd be willing."

"I'd like it a whole lot," he said, his eyes softening with gratitude. He frowned again. "She's been acting like a porcupine lately, so don't be offended if she seems a bit unfriendly." Cody hesitated, looked away and sighed. "Then again, she might be overly friendly. Just don't be shocked by anything she says or does, all right?"

"I won't be," Sherry promised. "I'm sure we'll get along just fine." She wasn't as confident as she sounded, but she found she liked Cody Bailman. It hadn't been easy for him to discuss such private matters with a stranger, a woman, no less, yet he'd put his concern for his daughter first. She was impressed.

"I found something the other day. I'm sure Heather didn't mean for me to see it. Frankly, it's got me worried."

"What was it?"

"A book. She had it tucked between the cushions in the sofa. It was one of those romance novels you women like so much. I tell you right now, it's got me concerned."

"Why?"

"Well, because I don't think it's a good idea for her to be clouding her head up with that sort of nonsense." He muttered something else, but Sherry didn't catch it. Apparently he didn't think highly of romance.

"I'll bring it up with her if you want," Sherry offered. "Of course, I won't let her know you found the book."

Cody stood. "I appreciate this, Miz . . ."

"Waterman. But please, call me Sherry."

"Sherry," he repeated. He held out his hand and she took it. Was it her imagination, or did he maintain contact a moment longer than necessary? Her gaze fell to their clasped hands, and he released her fingers as if he suddenly realized what he was doing. "It's been a pleasure."

"Thank you. Do you want to bring Heather in to see me tomorrow afternoon, or would you rather I paid a visit to your ranch?"

"Could you? It'd be best if this visit appeared casual-like. If Heather ever found out I was talking to anyone about her, she'd be madder than a mule with a mouthful of bees."

"I'll get directions from Mrs. Colson and be there shortly after lunch—say one o'clock?"

"Perfect."

Cody lingered at the door and seemed to assess her. "Are you thinking of sticking around Pepper?"

"I was hired last month but wasn't scheduled to start work for another two weeks. But it seems I'm starting early."

Sherry couldn't believe she'd said that. Until the minute Cody Bailman had walked in the door she'd been intent on demanding her two weeks. Now, she wasn't so sure.

"I'll see you tomorrow, then," Cody said, grinning broadly.

"Tomorrow," she agreed.

Still he stayed. "Might as well come by around lunchtime. The least I can do is feed you."

With a slight nod of her head, she accepted his offhand invitation.

The phone on the desk pealed, breaking the silence and the spell that seemed to have taken hold of them both. Then the ring was cut off. Apparently Mrs. Colson had picked it up.

As Cody was just about to leave, the receptionist burst through the door, a look of panic in her eyes. "That was Luke Johnson. Ellie's having labor pains, and he's scared to death he's gonna have to deliver that baby on his own. You'd better get over there quick as you can."

"Where?" Sherry demanded.

"Rattlesnake Ridge," Cody supplied. "Come on," he said gripping her elbow. "I'll drive you. You'd never find it on your own."

CHAPTER TWO

''RATTLESNAKE RIDGE?'' Sherry muttered under her breath as she hurried with Cody toward his pickup truck. He opened the passenger door and helped her inside. Although slender, Sherry wasn't the sort of female who generally required assistance, but her comparatively meager height—five foot five, as opposed to Cody's six-two—meant she needed help this time. The tires on his truck looked as if they belonged on a tanker trailer.

It was impossible to determine the color of the vehicle, and Sherry was convinced it hadn't been washed since it'd been driven off the showroom floor. Maybe, she thought, the dirt helped the rust hold the thing together.

Once she situated herself inside the cab, Cody raced around the front and leapt inside. His door made a cranking sound when he opened and closed it. He shoved the key into the ignition and the engine roared to life. She couldn't help but notice all the papers clipped to the dash; it looked as if he stored the majority of his paperwork there. She couldn't suppress a smile at his fingertip filing system.

''I'll need some things from my car,'' she told him. ''It's parked over by the café.'' Cody stopped on Main

Street, directly in front of her GEO and answered her unasked question.

"It's the only car I didn't recognize," he said as he opened the door and jumped down, then came around to give her a hand.

By the time Sherry was back in the pickup and fumbling with her seat belt, they were racing out of town.

Over the years Norah had written her long letters about life in Texas saying that the men here were as unique as the trucks they drove. Sherry had been amused and intrigued enough to move here herself. She was beginning to understand what Norah had meant about the men.

"I wish I'd talked to Luke myself," Cody muttered. He glanced at Sherry as if she were somehow to blame for his friend's discomfort. "That man's so besotted with Ellie he'd lose his head completely if anything ever happened to her."

Sherry grinned. "Isn't that the way a man *should* feel about his wife?"

Cody didn't answer right away. "Some men with some women, I suppose," he said several moments later as though it pained him to admit it.

"Are there really rattlesnakes out there on Rattlesnake Ridge?" Sherry asked conversationally.

Cody grinned. "In Texas we tend to call a spade a spade. We don't pretty up the truth, and the truth is there's rattlers on that ridge. Notice it ain't named Buttercup Hill."

"I see." She swallowed tightly. "Are snakes a real problem around here?"

"You afraid of snakes?" His gaze momentarily left the road.

"Not particularly," she said, trying to make her tone light. Norah hadn't said anything about snakes. "Tell me what you know about Ellie. Doc said she'd gone two weeks beyond her due date with the first pregnancy. Do you remember the baby's birth weight?"

Cody glanced at her again, as if puzzled by her prying.

"If I'm going to be delivering this baby, every bit of information is helpful," she said. "Is Ellie small and delicate?"

"Aren't all women?"

Sherry could see that Cody wasn't going to be much help. "What else can you tell me about her?"

"Well, she's real cute."

"Young?"

"Mid-twenties, maybe younger. Luke wasn't much interested in marriage until Ellie came to visit her grandparents a few years back. He took one look at her and he hasn't been the same since. I swear he walked around like a sick calf from the moment he met her." Cody frowned before he continued, "Unfortunately, his condition hasn't improved much since. It's been a long while since I've seen a man as smitten as Luke." He said this last part as if he had little patience with the emotion. "My bet is that Ellie's the calm one now."

"Her first pregnancy was normal?"

"I wouldn't know."

"Boy or girl?"

"Girl. Christina Lynn. Cute as a bug's ear, too."

"Was she a big baby?"

"Not that I recall, but then I wouldn't know much about that sort of thing."

"How old is Christina Lynn?"

"She must be a year or so." He paused. "Is that bad?"

"Why?" His question surprised her.

"Because you frowned."

Sherry hadn't realized she had. "No, it's just that they didn't wait long before Ellie became pregnant again."

"No, but if you want the truth, I don't think this one was planned any more than Christina Lynn was. As I said earlier, Luke's besotted. Got his head in the clouds where Ellie's concerned."

Sherry found that all rather endearing. She liked his terminology, too. Smitten, besotted. Here she was in her late twenties and no man had ever felt that way about her—nor she about any man. This was one of the reasons she'd decided to move away from Orchard Valley. If she stayed, she had the sinking feeling the rest of her life would have gone on just as it had been. She'd been content, but never excited. Busy, but bored. Liked, but not loved.

Her entire life had been spent in Orchard Valley, a small town where neighbors were friends and the sense of community was strong. It was one of the reasons Sherry had accepted the position in Pepper.

Norah had made the transition from Orchard Valley to Houston without a lot of difficulty, but Sherry wasn't sure she'd have done nearly as well. She didn't have a big-city mentality. But, Norah's letters about the Lone Star state had intrigued her, and if she was going to make a change, she couldn't see doing it by half measure. So she'd answered the agency's advertisement with a long letter and a detailed résumé. They phoned almost immediately, and she was hired so fast, without a personal interview, her head spun. She did learn from Dr. Colby Winston, Norah's brother-in-law, that her references had been checked and this eased her mind.

They'd been driving about twenty minutes when Cody braked suddenly to turn off the main road and onto a rugged dirt-and-gravel one. Sherry pitched forward, and without the restraint of the seat belt, would have slammed against the dash.

"You all right?"

"Sure," she said, a bit breathless. "How much farther?"

"Ten miles or so."

Sherry groaned inwardly and forced a smile. Even if they'd been driving at normal speed, the road would have been a challenge. Sherry felt like a yo-yo doing a round-the-world spin. Her body pitched one way and another, and she was forced to grip the seat with both hands.

When at last Cody pulled into the ranch yard, the road smoothed out. He eased to a stop in front of a two-story white house, which to Sherry looked like a desert oasis, standing out in a sort of warm welcome from the heat and barrenness. The windows were decorated with wide bright blue shutters, and brilliant red geraniums bloomed in the boxes out front. The wraparound porch was freshly painted. Sherry watched as the front door swung open and a tall, rangy cowman barreled out and down the steps.

"What took you so damn long?" he hollered. "El-lie's in pain."

Sherry was still fiddling with her seat belt when Cody opened the door for her. His hands fit snugly around her waist as he helped her down from the cab.

"Sherry, meet Luke," Cody said.

"Where's Doc?" Luke demanded.

"Fishing," Sherry explained, holding out her hand. "I'm Sherry Waterman and I—"

Luke's hand barely touched hers as his gaze moved accusingly to Cody, interrupting her introduction. "You brought some stranger out here for Ellie? Cody, this is my wife! You can't bring just anyone to—"

"I'm a midwife, as well as a physician's assistant," Sherry supplied. "I can do just about everything Dr. Lindsey does, including prescribe medication and de-liver babies. Now, where's your wife?"

"Cody?" Luke looked at his friend uncertainly.

"Do you want to deliver Ellie's baby yourself?" Cody asked him.

Luke went visibly pale and shook his head mutely.

"That's what I thought." Cody's hand cupped Sherry's elbow as he escorted her into the house. "You'll have to forgive Luke," he whispered. "As I said earlier, he's been screwy ever since he met Ellie."

The door led into the kitchen. A toddler was sitting in a high chair grinning happily and slamming a wooden spoon against the tray.

"Christina Lynn, I assume," Sherry said.

The toddler's face broke into a wide smile. At least Luke's daughter seemed pleased to see her.

"Where's Ellie?" Sherry asked Luke.

"Upstairs. Hurry, please!" Luke strode swiftly toward the staircase.

Sherry followed, taking the stairs two at a time, Cody right behind her.

When Sherry reached the hallway, Luke led the way into the master bedroom. Ellie was braced against the headboard, her eyes closed, her teeth gnawing on her lower lip. Her hand massaged her swollen abdomen as she breathed deeply in and out.

Luke fell to his knees and reached for her free hand, kissing her knuckles fervently. "They're here. There's nothing to worry about now."

Ellie acknowledged Sherry's and Cody's presence with an absent nod. Sherry waited until the contraction had ebbed before she asked, "How far apart are they?"

"Five minutes," Ellie said. "They started up hard, right after my water broke."

"How long ago was that?"

"An hour or so."

"I better check you, then." Sherry set her bag down at the foot of the bed and reached for a pair of rubber gloves.

"Cody?" Once again Luke pleaded for his friend's advice.

"Cody," said Ellie, "kindly keep my big oaf of a husband entertained for a while." She motioned toward the door. "Make him tend to Christina Lynn—she shouldn't be left alone, anyway. Whatever you do, keep him out of this room."

"But, Ellie, you need me!" Luke protested.

"Not right now I don't, honey. Cody, do as I say and keep Luke out of here."

Cody virtually pushed Luke out of the room. After the pair had left, Ellie looked to Sherry. "Whoever you are, welcome. I couldn't be more pleased to see another woman."

Sherry smiled. "Sherry Waterman. I'm new to Pepper. Doc was so excited by my arrival that he took off fishing. He said you weren't due for another couple of weeks."

"I'm not, but then we miscalculated with Christina Lynn, too."

"I'll wash my hands and be right back." By the time Sherry returned, Ellie was in the middle of another contraction. She waited until Ellie had relaxed, then adjusted her pillows to make her as comfortable as possible.

"How am I doing?" Ellie asked after the pain receded. Her brow was covered with a thin sheen of perspiration. She licked her dry lips.

"You're doing just great," Sherry told her, wiping the woman's face with a wet rag.

"How much longer will it take?"

"A while," Sherry told her gently. "Maybe several hours yet."

Ellie's shoulders sagged. "I was afraid of that."

Twenty minutes later, Cody appeared after knocking lightly on the bedroom door. "How's everything going up here?"

"Great," Sherry assured him. "Ellie's an excellent patient."

"I wish I could say the same for Luke. Is there anything I can get you?"

"Pillows and a cassette player." At his frown, she elaborated, "Soothing music will help relax Ellie during the contractions. I have tapes with me."

Cody nodded and looked at Ellie. "Don't worry about Christina Lynn. She's in her crib now and sound asleep. I phoned the ranch, and our housekeeper's staying with Heather, so everything's been taken care of at my end."

"Whatever you do, keep Luke out of here," Ellie said. "You'd think I was the only woman ever to suffer labor pains. He was a wreck by the time Christina Lynn was born. Doc Lindsey had to spend more time with him than me."

"I'll keep him in line," replied Cody, ducking back out of the room.

Sherry remembered more than one birth where the father required full-time attention. It always warmed her that men could be so greatly affected by the birth of their children.

"Talk to me," Ellie requested before the next powerful contraction gripped her body.

Sherry told the woman about her introduction to the good people in Pepper. About meeting Mayor Bowie and Doc Lindsey and Billy Bob. Ellie laughed softly, then as the pain came again, she rolled onto her side and Sherry massaged the tightness from the small of her back, all the while murmuring encouragingly.

"I'm a transplant myself," Ellie spoke when she could. "I was a college sophomore when I came here to visit my grandparents. They've lived in Pepper for as long as I can remember. I only intended on staying a few days, but then I met Luke. I swear he was the most pigheaded, most ill-behaved man I'd ever known. I told myself I never wanted to have anything to do with the likes of him. To be truthful, I was a bit sweet on Cody Bailman, but only at first."

"Obviously your opinion of Luke changed."

"My sweet Luke. You've never seen anyone more crusty on the outside and more gentle on the inside. I'll never forget the afternoon he proposed. I'd decided to drive back home to Dallas—good grief, I'd spent two weeks longer than I'd originally intended. Luke didn't want me to leave, but I really didn't have any choice. I had a job waiting for me and was signed up for classes in the fall. Grandma sent me off with enough food to last me into the following month."

Sherry chuckled and waited for Ellie to work her way through the next contraction.

"I was five miles out of town when I saw this man on a horse galloping after me as if catching me was a matter of life or death. It was Luke." She shook her head remembering. "When I pulled over to the side of the road, he jumped off his horse, removed his glove and fell to one knee and proposed. I knew then and there I wasn't ever going to find a man who would love me as much as Luke Johnson. Suddenly nothing mattered without him, not anymore. I know my parents were disappointed I didn't finish college, but I'm happy and that's what counts."

"You don't mind living so far away from town?"

"At first, just a little. Now I'm happy about it."

"That's wonderfully romantic story."

Ellie smiled. "Is there a special man in your life?"

Sherry exhaled slowly. "I've never fallen in love. Oh, I had a few crushes, the way we all do when we're young. I dated a doctor for a while, but both of us knew it wasn't going anywhere." Sherry smiled to herself remembering how difficult it was for Colby Winston to admit he was in love with Valerie Bloomfield.

In the hours that followed, Cody came up to check on their progress twice more and give a report of his own. Luke, he said, had worn a path in the living-room carpet pacing back and forth, but thus far, Cody had been able to restrain him from racing up the stairs. He doubted that Luke would have much hair left though before the ordeal was over; he'd jerked his hands through the thick mop so many times there were grooves in his hairline.

"He loves me," Ellie said softly.

When Sherry walked Cody to the bedroom door, he asked quietly, "Will it be much longer? Luke's a mess."

"Another couple of hours."

Cody nodded and his eyes briefly held hers. "I'm glad you're here." He turned and headed down the stairs. A surge of emotion gripped her, but she wasn't sure how to read it. All she knew was that she felt *alive,* acutely sensitive to sounds and colors, and she had the impression Cody experienced the same thing.

"I'm glad you're here, too," Ellie said from behind her.

Sherry moved back to the bed. "Doc would have done just as well."

"Perhaps, but it helps that you're a woman."

The second stage of labor arrived shortly after midnight, and Ellie arched against the bed at the strength of her contractions, panting in between. Sherry coached her as she had so many others. And then, at last, with a shout of triumph, Ellie delivered a strong, squalling son.

The baby was barely in his mother's arms when the door burst open and Luke barged into the room.

"A son, Luke," Ellie whispered. "We have a son."

Luke knelt beside the bed and stared down at the angry infant in his wife's arms. The baby was a bright shade of pink, his legs and arms kicking in protest. His eyes were closed and he was yelling for all his worth. "He looks just like you when you get mad," Ellie told her husband.

Luke nodded and Sherry noticed his eyes were bright with tears as he bent forward and kissed his son's wrinkled brow. Then he gently placed his hand over Ellie's cheek and kissed her. "Never again," he vowed. "Our family's complete now."

Ellie's eyes drifted shut. "That's what you said after Christina Lynn was born."

"True," Luke admitted, "but that was because I couldn't bear to see you suffer again. This time it's for me. I don't think I could go through this another time. And, I nearly lost my best friend."

"You were a long way from that, partner," Cody said from the doorway.

"I don't care. Two children are plenty, understand, Ellie? I know you said you'd like four, but I won't hear of it. You agree with me now, don't you?"

Sherry moved behind the big, rangy cattleman and looked down at Ellie. "You're exhausted. You need some sleep." Gently lifting the baby from her arms, Sherry placed him in a soft blanket, marveling at the perfectly formed tiny person in her hands.

"Come on," Cody urged Luke. "It's time to celebrate. Let's break open that bottle of expensive scotch you've been saving."

"She's going to do it, you know," Luke said to no one in particular. "That woman knows I can't refuse her a damn thing. Before I even figure out how it happened, we're going to have four young ones running around this house."

Sherry finished her duties and found Luke and Cody in the living room each holding a shot of whiskey. "Ellie and Philip are sound asleep," she assured them.

"Philip," Luke repeated slowly, and a brightness came into his eyes. "She decided to name him Philip, after all."

"A family name?" Cody asked him.

Luke shrugged. "Actually, it's mine. I never much cared for it as a kid and dropped it when I entered school, insisting everyone call me by my middle name."

"Ellie says your son looks like a Philip," Sherry put in.

A wide grin split Luke's face. "I think she's right—he does." He looked down into the amber liquid in his glass. "A son. I've got myself a son."

Sherry smiled, then found herself yawning. It had been a long day. She'd been up since dawn, not wanting to travel in the worst heat of the day, and now it was well past two in the morning.

"Come on," Cody said, setting his glass down, "I'd better drive you back into town."

Sherry nodded and covered her mouth when yet another wide yawn escaped. She was weary through and through.

"Thank you," Luke said, his eyes bright. He took her limp hand and pumped it several times to show his gratitude. He seemed to have forgiven her for being a stranger.

"I'll be in touch with you both tomorrow," Sherry promised. "Ellie did a beautiful job with this baby."

"I know." Luke dropped his gaze as if embarrassed by his behavior earlier. "I knew the minute I saw that woman I was going to love her. What I didn't know was how damn lucky I was that I convinced her to marry me."

"From what Ellie told me, she considers herself the lucky one." Luke grinned hugely at Sherry's words.

"Come on, Sherry, you're beat," Cody said, cupping her elbow. "Good night, Luke."

"Night." Luke walked with them to the front door. "Ellie's mother is on her way and should be here by morning. She'll be a big help. But thanks again."

By the time Sherry was inside Cody's truck, she was dead on her feet. She dreaded the long, rough drive back into town, but there was no help for it.

"SHERRY." Her name seemed to come from a long distance away. The bottom of a well, perhaps. It was then that she realized she'd been asleep.

She'd meant to stay awake, but apparently she was more tired than she realized, for she'd slept through that dreadful ten miles before they hit the main road. Cody must have driven the stretch with infinite care.

To compound her sense of disorientation, she found her head neatly tucked against his shoulder. It felt warm and comfortable there, she wasn't inclined to move.

"We're in town already?" she asked, slowly opening her eyes.

"No. I couldn't see taking you all the way into Pepper when you're so tired."

Sherry straightened and looked around. They were parked outside a barn beside an enormous brick house with arched windows on the main floor and four gables jetting out from the second. The place, which was illuminated by several outdoor lights, resembled something from a prime-time soap opera.

"Where are we?" she asked.

"My place, the Lucky Horseshoe. I figured you could spend what's left of the night here. I'll drive you back into town first thing in the morning."

Sherry was too tired to argue, not that she wanted to. She liked and trusted this cattleman, and when he came around to help her from the cab, she found herself almost eager to feel his hands on her waist again.

Cody helped her down, and if he was feeling any of what Sherry was, he didn't show it.

"I hope I didn't make a pest of myself falling asleep on you that way," she said.

He mumbled something she couldn't quite make out. But apparently she hadn't troubled him. He led the way into the big country kitchen, turning on lights as he went.

Without asking, he took down two large glasses from the cupboard and filled them with milk from the refrigerator. "You didn't have any dinner."

Sherry had to stop a moment and think about it. He was right. She hadn't had anything since the cheeseburger and pie at lunchtime. It surprised her to realize she wasn't the least bit hungry.

"Here," he said, handing her the glass of milk. "This'll tide you over till breakfast."

"Thanks."

He pulled out a chair for her, then twisted the one across from it around and straddled it. They didn't seem to have a lot to say to each other, yet the room was charged with electricity.

"So," he ventured, "you're planning to stay in Pepper?"

Sherry nodded. She liked the gruff quality of his voice. She liked his face, too, not that he was turn-her-bones-to-water handsome. His features were tough and masculine, browned by the sun and creased with experience, some of it hard, she guessed.

"You'll like it here. Pepper's a good town."

Everything about Cody Bailman fascinated her. A few strands of thick dark hair fell over his high forehead, giving him a little-boy look. It was so appealing that Sherry had to resist leaning forward and brushing the hair away.

"The guest bedroom's upstairs," Cody said abruptly, and stood. He drained the last of his milk in three gulps and set the empty glass in the sink.

Sherry drank the last of her own and stood, too. She'd forgotten how tired she was.

"This way," Cody whispered, leading her up the gently curving stairway off the entryway.

Sherry paused and glanced around at the expensive furnishings, the antiques and works of art. "Your home is lovely."

''Thanks.''

Sherry followed him to the top of the stairs and then to the room at the far end of the hallway. He opened the door and cursed under his breath.

''Is something wrong?'' Sherry asked.

''The bed isn't made up. Heather had a friend stay here last night and she'd promised to change the sheets and make up the bed herself. Apparently she forgot. Listen, I'll make do in here and you can sleep in my room. Janey, our housekeeper, changed the sheets just today.''

''That isn't necessary,'' she protested. It would only take a matter of minutes to assemble the bed.

''You're dead on your feet,'' Cody returned. ''Here.'' He reached for her hand and led her down to the other end of the hallway.

Had she possessed the energy, Sherry would have continued to protest, but Cody's evaluation of her state was pretty accurate.

''Call me if you need anything, and don't argue, understand?''

Sherry nodded.

Whether it was by impulse or design, she didn't know, but before he turned away, Cody leaned down and casually brushed her lips with his.

They both seemed taken back by the quick exchange. Neither spoke for what seemed the longest moment of Sherry's life. Her pulse was pounding wildly in her throat, and Cody reached out and pressed his fingertip to the frantic throbbing. Then, before she could encourage or dissuade him, he bent his head and brushed her mouth with his a second time.

Her moist lips quivered beneath the gentle contact. He moved toward her and she toward him, and soon they were wrapped in each other's arms. The kiss took on an exploring, demanding quality as if this moment was all they'd be granted and they'd best make the most they could of it.

Sherry nearly staggered when he released her. "Good night, Sherry," he said, then she watched as his giant strides ate up the length of the hallway. He paused when he reached the opposite end and turned back to look at her. Even from this distance, Sherry could read the dilemma in his eyes. He didn't want to be attracted to her, hadn't wanted to kiss her, and now that he had, he wasn't at all sure what to do about it.

Sherry was experiencing many of those same feelings herself. She opened the door and stepped inside his room, angry with herself for not insisting on the guest room. For everything about these quarters shouted of Cody. From the basalt fireplace to the large four-poster bed.

She pulled back the sheets and undressed. She'd thought she'd be asleep before her head hit the pillow, but she was wrong. She tossed and turned till dawn, the image of Cody standing at the end of the hallway staring at her as if he regretted ever having met her burned in her brain. At last she fell into a troubled sleep.

"HOT DAMN."

Sherry opened one eye and saw a pretty girl of about twelve, dressed in jeans and a red plaid shirt, standing just inside the doorway. Dark braids dangled across her shoulders.

"Hot damn," the girl repeated, smiling as if it was Christmas morning and she'd found Santa sitting under the tree waiting for her.

Sherry levered herself up on one elbow and squinted against the light. "Hello."

"Howdy," the girl greeted eagerly with a wide grin.

"What time is it?" Sherry rubbed her eyes. It seemed she'd only been asleep a matter of minutes. If it hadn't been rude to do so, she would have fallen back against the thick down pillow and covered her face with the sheet.

"Eight-thirty. Where's Dad?"

"Uh . . . you're Heather?"

"So he mentioned me, did he?" she asked gleefully. The girl walked into the room and leapt onto the mattress, making it bounce.

"I think you have the wrong impression of what's going on here," Sherry felt obliged to tell the girl.

"You're in my dad's bed, aren't you? That tells me everything I need to know. Besides, you're the first woman I've seen him bring home. I think I got the picture. How'd you two meet?" She tucked her knees up under her chin and looped her arms around them, preparing herself for a lengthy explanation.

"Heather!" Cody's voice boomed from the end of the hallway.

"In here!" she shouted back with enough force to cause Sherry to grimace.

Cody appeared as if by magic two seconds later, his large frame filling the doorway.

"Dad," Heather said with a disappointed sigh, "you've been holding out on me."

CHAPTER THREE

"GEE, DAD, WHEN'S the wedding?"

"Heather!" Cody ground out furiously. He looked as if he'd dressed in a hurry. He was in jeans and barefoot, and his Western-style shirt was left open, exposing his hard chest and abdomen, and an attractive spattering of dark, curly hair.

"But, Dad, you've comprom—" she faltered "—ruined your friend's reputation! Surely you intend on making an honest woman of her."

Sherry laughed. She couldn't help it, although it was clear Cody wasn't amused by his daughter badgering. Heather's clear blue eyes sparkled with mischief.

"So," the girl continued, "how long has this been going on?"

"You will apologize to Miz Waterman," Cody insisted, his voice hard as cable.

"Sorry, Miz Waterman," Heather said. She didn't sound at all contrite. "I take it you're new in town?"

Sherry nodded and thrust out her hand. "Call me Sherry. I'll be working with Doc Lindsey."

"Wow. That's great. Real great!"

"I was with Ellie Johnson last night," Sherry said.

"Ellie had her baby?" Heather's excited gaze shot to her father.

"A boy. They named him Philip," Cody answered.

Heather slapped her hand against the mattress. "Hot damn! Luke never said anything, but I know he was hoping for a boy. But then, Luke's so crazy about Ellie he'd have been happy with a litter of kittens."

Cody rubbed his forehead. "We didn't get back to the house till after two. The guest bed wasn't made up." He looked accusingly at his daughter.

"Oops." Heather slapped her fingers against her lips. "I said I'd do that, didn't I? Sorry about that."

Sherry cleared her throat. "Uh, I'd better see about getting back to town." With Doc gone she was responsible for any medical emergency that might arise. Not that she intended to be manipulated into staying. She still intended on taking the time entitled to her, with or without the Sheriff's approval.

"You want me to see if Slim can drive her for you?" Heather asked her father.

"I'll do it," Cody said casually, turning away from them. "But first we'll have breakfast."

"Breakfast," Heather repeated meaningly. She wiggled her eyebrows up and down several times before climbing off the bed. "He's going to drive you back into town himself," she added, grinning at Sherry. Her smile grew wider and the sparkle in her eyes was bright enough to light a fire. "Yup," she said. "My dad's sweet on you. Real sweet. This could be downright interesting. It's about time he started listening to me."

"I . . . We only met yesterday," Sherry explained.

"So?"

"I mean, well, isn't it a little soon to be making those kind of judgments."

"Nope." Heather plopped herself down on the edge of the bed once more. "How do you feel about him? He's kinda handsome, don't you think?"

"Ah..."

"You'll have to be patient with him, though. Dad tends to be a little dumb when it comes to dealing with women. He's got a lot to learn, but between the two of us, we should be able to train him, don't you think?"

Sherry had gotten the impression from talking to Cody that Heather was a timid child struggling with her identity. Ha! This girl didn't have a timid bone in her body.

"I love romance," Heather said on a long drawn-out sigh. She looked behind her to be sure no one was listening, then lowered her voice. "I've been waiting a long time for Dad to come to his senses about marrying again. My mom died when I was only two, so I hardly even remember her, and—"

"Heather, your father and I've only just met," Sherry reminded her. "I'm afraid you're leaping to conclusions that could be embarrassing to both your father and me."

The girl's face fell. "You think so? It's just that I'm so anxious for Dad to find a wife. If he doesn't hurry, I'll be grown up before there're any more babies. In case you haven't guessed, I really like babies. Besides, it's not much fun being an only child." She hesitated and seemed to change her mind. "Sometimes it is, but sometimes it isn't. You know what I mean?"

Sherry would have answered, given the chance, but Heather immediately began speaking again.

"You like him, don't you?"

Sherry pushed the hair away from her face with both hands. She didn't need to look in a mirror to know her cheeks were aflame. "You're father's a very nice man, but as I said before—"

"Heather!" Cody boomed again.

"He wants me to leave you alone," Heather translated with a grimace. "But we'll have a chance to talk later, right?"

"Uh...sure." Sherry was beginning to feel dizzy, as if she'd been caught up in a whirlwind and wasn't exactly sure when she would land—or where.

It was impossible not to like Cody's daughter. She was vibrant and refreshing and fun. And not the least bit timid.

"Great. I'll talk to you soon, then."

"Right."

Fifteen minutes later, Sherry walked down the stairs and into the kitchen. Cody and Heather were sitting at the table and a middle-aged woman with thick gray braids looped on top of her head smiled a warm welcome.

"Hello," Sherry said to the small gathering.

"Sherry, this is Janey," Cody said. "She does the cooking and the housekeeping around here."

Sherry nodded when introduced and noticed the eager look exchanged between Heather and the cook. Heather, it appeared, hadn't stopped smiling from the moment she'd discovered Sherry sleeping in her father's bed. The housekeeper looked equally pleased.

"Janey's been around forever," Heather explained as she stretched across the table to spear a hot pancake with her fork.

Janey chuckled. "I'm a bit younger than Heather believes, but not by much. Now sit down and I'll bring you some cakes hot off the griddle."

Cody didn't have much to say during their breakfast, although Sherry was certain he was convinced bringing her to the ranch was a big mistake.

Breakfast was delicious. Cody didn't contribute much to the conversation, not that Sherry blamed him. Anything he said was sure to be open to speculation. A comment on the weather would no doubt send Heather into a soliloquy about summer being the perfect time of year to have a wedding. The girl seemed determined to do whatever she could to arrange a marriage for her father. Sherry's presence only worsened the situation.

After they'd finished eating, Cody said he needed a few minutes to check with his men. Sherry took the opportunity to phone the Johnson ranch and see how Ellie and the baby were doing. She spoke to Luke who said that everything was well in hand, especially since Ellie's mother had arrived that morning. Once again, he thanked Sherry for her help.

"You ready?" Cody asked when she hung up the phone.

"All set. Just let me say goodbye to Janey."

When Sherry walked into the yard a few minutes later, Cody was waiting for her. Heather had gone with her, and the girl paused when she saw her father standing outside the pickup. "You aren't driving her back in that old thing, are you? Dad, that truck's disgusting."

"Yes, I am," Cody said in a voice that defied arguing. It didn't stop Heather, however.

"But Sherry's special. I'd think you'd want to take her in the Caddie."

"It's fine, Heather," Sherry insisted, opening the door of the truck herself. Unfortunately she was at least six inches too short to boost herself into the cab. Cody's aid seemed to come grudgingly. Maybe he regretted not accepting Heather's advice about which car to drive, she thought.

Sherry waved to the girl as they pulled out of the yard. Heather, with a good deal of drama, crossed her hands over her heart and collapsed, as if struck by how very sweet romance could be. With some effort, Sherry controlled her amusement.

Cody's ranch was huge. They'd been driving silently for what seemed like miles and were still on his spread. She asked him a couple of questions, to which he responded with little more than a grunt. Apparently he was something of a grouch when he didn't get a good night's sleep.

About ten minutes outside of town he cleared his throat as if he had something important to announce. "I hope you didn't take anything Heather said seriously."

"You mean about your making an honest woman of me?"

He snorted. "Yes."

"No, of course I didn't."

"Good."

He was so serious it was all she could do not to laugh.

"The kiss, too," he added, his brow folded into a thick frown.

"Kisses," she reminded him, making sure he understood there had been more than one.

Despite her restless sleep, Sherry honestly hadn't given the matter much thought. She did so now, concluding that they'd both been exhausted and rummy, high on the emotional aftermath of the birth of Philip and the roles they'd each played in the small drama. Being attracted to each other was completely understandable, given those circumstances. The kisses had been a sort of celebration for the new life they'd helped usher into the world. There hadn't been anything sexual about them, had there?

"Let's call them a breech of good judgment," Cody suggested.

"All right." That wasn't how Sherry would define them, but Cody seemed comfortable with the explanation—and pleased with her understanding.

They remained silent for the rest of the trip, and Sherry grew thoughtful. She found she agreed with him in principle. Their evening together had been a step out of time. Nevertheless, disappointment spread through her. It was as though she'd been standing on the brink of a great discovery and had suddenly learned it was all a hoax.

Her entire romantic career had followed a similar sorry pattern. Just when she thought perhaps she'd found her life's partner in Colby Winston, she discovered she experienced no great emotion toward him. Certainly nothing like what Ellie had described to her.

Sherry knew precious little of love. Four years earlier, she'd watched the three Bloomfield sisters back home in Orchard Valley find love, all within the space of one short summer. Love had seemed explosive and chaotic with each sister. Valerie and Colby had both been caught unaware, each fighting their attraction and each other. Sherry had stood by and watched the man she'd once seriously dated herself fall head over heels in love. She knew then that this was what she wanted for herself.

Then Valerie's sister Steffie had returned from Italy. She and Charles were brought back together after a three-year separation and they, too, had seemed unprepared for the strength of their feelings. They were married only a matter of weeks after Valerie and Colby.

But the Bloomfield sister who had surprised Sherry the most was Norah. They'd been schoolmates, sharing the same interests and often the same friends. A smile never failed to appear on Sherry's face whenever she thought of Norah and Rowdy. The lanky millionaire Texan hadn't known what hit him when he fell for Norah, and the amusing thing was Norah hadn't, either. All of Orchard Valley had seemed to hold its collective breath awaiting the outcome of their romance. But Norah and Rowdy made the ideal couple, Sherry had thought. Nothing, outside of love, would have convinced Norah to leave Orchard Valley.

In the years since Norah had left Oregon, Sherry had been busy studying and working toward her degree, too absorbed in her goal to find time for relationships. But now she was ready. She wanted the love her friends had found, the excitement, the thrill of finding that special someone, of being courted and treasured. She was looking for a man who felt about her the way Luke felt about Ellie. She wanted a man to look at her the way Colby Winston looked at Valerie Bloomfield.

Cody eased the truck to a stop behind Sherry's GEO. Sherry unbuckled the seat belt and reached for her purse and medical bag.

"I really appreciate the ride," she said, holding out her hand for him to shake.

"You're welcome." He briefly took her hand, then leapt from the cab and came around to help her down. When his hands came to encircle her waist, his eyes captured hers. For the longest moment she didn't move, couldn't move, as if his touch had caused a strange paralysis. But when he shifted his gaze away, she placed her hands on his shoulders and allowed him to lift her to the ground. As she met his gaze again, she read surprise and a twinge of regret there.

Cody eased away from her, and Sherry watched as an invisible barrier was erected between them. Irritation seemed to flicker through him. "I'm not going to apologize for kissing you last night," he said softly.

"But you regret it?"

"Yes, more so now than before."

The harsh edge to his voice took her by surprise. "Why?" The word was little more than a throaty whisper.

"Because it's going to be damn difficult to keep from doing it again." With that, he stalked back to the driver's side of the pickup, climbed in and roared off.

Sherry got into her car and drove the short distance to the clinic, parking in the small lot behind the building. When she walked around and went in the front door, Mrs. Colson broke into a wide smile. "Welcome back."

"Thanks. Ellie had a beautiful baby boy."

"So I heard. Word spreads fast around these parts. Ellie claims she'll never have another baby without you there. She thinks you're the best thing to happen to Pepper since we voted in sewers last November."

Sherry laughed. "I don't suppose you've heard from Doc Lindsey?"

"Yes. He called this morning to see if everything was working out."

Sherry was relieved. At least the physician had some sense of responsibility. "I want to talk to him when he phones in again."

"No problem. He wants to talk to you, too. Apparently there's a misunderstanding—you weren't scheduled to begin work for another two weeks."

"That's what I've been trying to tell everyone," Sherry said emphatically. "I made the mistake of driving through town, and everyone assumed that because I was here I was starting right away."

Mrs. Colson fiddled with a folder from the file drawer, pulling out a sheet of paper and glancing through its contents. "Doc's right. It's here as plain as day. So, why *are* you here so early?"

Briefly Sherry wondered if a megahorn would help the good people of Pepper hear her. "I was just passing through on my way to Houston," she explained patiently. "Mayor Bowie assumed I was here to stay and so did Doc. Before I could stop him, he was out the door with his fishing pole in hand."

"You should've said something."

Sherry resisted the urge to scream. "I tried, but no one would listen."

"Well, Doc told me to tell you he'll be back in town sometime this afternoon. He claims the fish don't bite this early in the season, anyway."

"I'll need to call my friends and tell them I'm going to be late," Sherry said.

"Sure, go right ahead. The town'll pay for the call."

Sherry decided to wait until she'd showered and changed clothes before she contacted Norah. It was midmorning before she felt human again.

"I'm in Pepper," Sherry explained once she had Norah on the line. "It's a long story, but I won't be able to leave until later this afternoon, which will put me in Houston sometime late tomorrow."

"That's no problem," Norah was quick to assure her. "I'm so pleased you're coming! I've missed you, Sherry."

"I've missed you, too."

"So how do you like Texas so far?" Norah wanted to know.

Given Sherry's circumstances, it was an unfair question. "I haven't been here long enough to form an opinion. The natives seem friendly enough, and with a little practice I think I'll be able to pick up the language."

Norah chuckled. "Oh, Sherry, I am so looking forward to seeing you! Don't worry, I've decided to give you a crash course on the state and the people once you arrive. You're going to love it—just the way I do."

Sherry didn't comment on that. "How's Rowdy?" she said, instead.

"Busy as ever. I swear that man runs circles around me, but that's all right. It's me he comes home to every night and me he sits across the dinner table from, and me he loves. He's such a good father and an even better husband.''

"Val and Steffie send their love. Your dad, too.''

"Talking to you makes me miss them even more. Rowdy promised me we'd fly to Orchard Valley sometime this fall, but I doubt Dad's going to wait that long. I half expect him to drop by for a visit before the end of the summer.''

Sherry chuckled. "Well, at least I'll be there before he is.''

"It wouldn't matter,'' Norah said. "You're welcome anytime.''

Sherry felt a lot better after talking to her friend. But Norah sounded so happy she couldn't quite squelch a feeling of envy. Norah and Rowdy had two small children and were looking into adopting two more. Norah had always been a natural with children. Sherry never did understand why her friend with her flair with youngsters, hadn't chosen pediatrics.

In an effort to help the time pass till Doc's arrival, Sherry read through several medical journals in his office. When she looked up, it was well past noon.

Mrs. Colson stuck her head in the door, "Do you want me to order you some lunch?'' she asked.

"No thanks.'' Her impatience for Doc to arrive had completely destroyed her appetite.

"I'm going to order a salad for myself. The Yellow Rose is real good about running it over here to me. You sure I can't talk you into anything?''

"I'm sure.''

Donna Jo stopped off fifteen minutes later with a chef salad and plopped herself down on a chair in the reception area. Mrs. Colson was behind the counter, and Sherry was sitting on another chair with her purse and suitcase all ready to go. "The Cattlemen's Association's in town for lunch," Donna Jo explained to the receptionist, removing her shoe and massaging her sore foot. She eyed Sherry with the same curiosity she had a day earlier. "I hear you delivered Ellie's baby last night."

Word had indeed gotten around. Sherry nodded.

"You must have spent the night out there with her and Luke, because Mayor Bowie came into the café this morning looking for you. You weren't at the clinic."

"Actually, Cody Bailman drove me over to his house."

"You stayed the night at Cody's?" Donna Jo asked. Both the waitress's and Mrs. Colson's interest was piqued.

"It was after two by the time I finished. I was exhausted, and so was Cody." She certainly didn't want to give the two the wrong impression. "Nothing happened. I mean, nothing that was, uh . . ." She gave up trying to find the words. "Cody was the perfect gentleman."

"Isn't he always?" Donna Jo winked at Mrs. Colson.

"Is there something wrong about my spending the night at Cody's?"

"Not in the least," Mrs. Colson was quick to assure her. "Cody's a gentleman."

"As much of a gentleman as any Texan gets," Donna Jo amended. "Martha, are you going to tell her, or am I?"

"Tell me what?" Sherry said.

Donna Jo and Mrs. Colson shared a significant look.

"What?" Sherry demanded again.

"I don't think so," Mrs. Colson said thoughtfully after a long moment. "She'll find out soon enough on her own."

Donna Jo nodded. "You're right."

"What will I find out on my own?" Sherry tried a third time, but again her question was ignored.

"Martha here tells me you're bent on leaving town," the waitress said conversationally. "Stop in at the café on your way out and I'll pack you a lunch to take along. You might not be hungry now, but you will be later."

"Thanks, I'll do that."

Doc arrived around two that afternoon, looking tired and disgruntled. "I've been up since before dawn," he muttered. "It didn't make sense that I wasn't reeling in fifteen-inchers until I realized it was too early in the month."

"I'll be back in less than two weeks," Sherry promised, "and next time the fish are sure to be biting."

"I hope so," Doc grumbled. "You might've said something about arriving early, you know."

Sherry nearly had to swallow her tongue to keep from reminding him she'd done everything but throw herself in front of his truck to keep him from leaving.

Sherry had almost passed the café when she remembered her promise to Donna Jo and pulled to a stop. The waitress was right; she should take something to eat with her, including several cold sodas. Already it was unmercifully hot. She chuckled, remembering Donna Jo's remark that the ones who escaped to Colorado for the summer weren't real Texans. Apparently folks were supposed to stay in Texas and suffer.

The café was nearly empty. Sherry took a seat at the counter and reached for the menu.

"What'll you have?" Donna Jo asked.

"Let's see ... A turkey sandwich with tomato and lettuce, a bag of chips and five diet sodas, all to go."

Donna Jo went into the kitchen to tell the chef. When she came back out her eyes brightened. "Howdy, Cody."

"Howdy." Cody slipped onto the stool next to Sherry and ordered coffee.

"Hi," he said, edging up his Stetson with his index finger as if to get a better look at her.

"Hi." It was silly to feel shy with him, but Sherry did. A little like she had in junior high when Wayne Pierce, on whom she'd had a crush, sat next to her in the school lunchroom. Her mouth went dry and she felt incapable of making conversation.

"I was wondering if I'd run into you this afternoon."

"Cody's in town for the local cattlemen's meeting," Donna Jo explained as she placed a beige ceramic mug full of steaming coffee in front of Cody.

"Doc's back," Sherry said, although she wasn't certain he understood the significance. "He said the fishing was terrible, but then, it generally is about now."

He shrugged, not agreeing or disagreeing with her. "You're having a rather late lunch, aren't you?"

Donna Jo set a brown paper bag on the counter along with the tab. "I was planning to eat on the road," Sherry said, thanking Donna Jo with a smile. She slipped her purse strap over her shoulder and opened the zipper to take out her wallet.

A frown crowded Cody's features. "You're leaving?"

"For Houston."

His frown deepened. "So soon?"

"I'll be back in a couple of weeks." She slid off the stool and was surprised when Cody slapped some coins on the counter and followed her to the register.

"Actually I was hoping to talk to you," he said, holding open the café door for her.

"Oh?" She headed for her car.

Cody followed. "Yeah, it's about what I said this morning." His eyes refused to meet hers. "I was thinking about it on my way back to the ranch, and I realized I must have sounded pretty arrogant about the whole thing."

"I didn't notice," Sherry lied, but it was only a small one. She found it rather charming that he wanted to correct the impression he'd made.

"It's just that Heather's on this kick, but you were so terrific with Ellie and everything else."

"We both agreed it was a lapse in judgment," she reminded him. "So let's just forget it ever happened."

He jammed his fingers into his pockets as Sherry opened her car door. "I wish I could," he said so low Sherry wasn't sure she heard him correctly.

"Pardon?" she said, looking up to him and making a feeble attempt at a smile.

"Nothing," he said gruffly. "I didn't say anything."

"You wish you could what?" she pressed, refusing to allow him off lightly.

He looked away from her and his wide shoulders moved up and down with a labored sigh. "I wish I could forget!" he said forcefully. "There. Are you happy now?"

"No," she returned softly. "I'm confused."

"So am I. I like you, Sherry. I don't know why, but I do, and I don't mind telling you it scares the living daylights out of me. The last time I was this attracted to a woman I was—" he stopped and rubbed the side of his jaw—"a hell of a lot younger than I am now. And you're leaving."

"But I'll be back." The rush to reach Houston at the earliest possible moment left her. Nothing appealed to her more than exploring what was happening between her and Cody Bailman at this moment.

"But you won't be back for two weeks." He made it sound like an eternity. His face tightened. "By the time you're back it won't be the same."

"We don't know that."

"I do," he said with certainty.

Sherry was torn. "Are you asking me to stay?"

His nostrils flared at the question. "No," he said forcefully, and then more softly, "No." He moved a step closer to her. "Aw, what the hell," he muttered crossly. He reached for her, wrapped his arm around her waist, dragged her toward him and kissed her soundly.

Tentatively, shyly, her lips opened to his until the kiss blossomed into something wanting and wonderful. At last he pulled away slightly and sighed. "There," he said, his breath warm against her face. "Now go, before I make an even bigger fool of myself."

But Sherry wasn't sure that she was capable of moving, let alone driving several hundred miles. She blinked and tried to catch her breath.

"Why'd you do that?" she demanded, pressing her fingertips to her lips.

"Damned if I know," Cody admitted, sounding none too pleased with himself.

Sherry understood the reason for his consternation when she looked around her. It seemed the entire town of Pepper, Texas, had stopped midmotion to stare at them. A couple of men loitering outside the hardware store were staring. Several curious faces filled the window at the Yellow Rose, including Donna Jo's. The waitress, in fact, looked downright excited and gave Sherry a thumbs-up.

"We've done it now," Cody muttered, staring down at her as if she was to blame. "Everyone's going to be talking."

"I'd like to remind you I wasn't the one who started the kissing."

"Yeah, but you sure enjoyed it."

"Well, this is just fine, isn't it," she said, glad for an excuse to be on her way. "I'm outta here. Tossing her lunch bag onto the passenger seat, she slipped inside the car.

"Sherry, dammit, don't leave yet."

"Why? What else have you planned?"

"Okay, okay, I shouldn't have kissed you, I'll be the first to agree." He rubbed his hand along the back of his neck as if considering his words. "As I said before, I like you."

"You have a funny way of showing it."

He closed his eyes and nodded. "Already I've made a mess of this, and I haven't even known you for a whole day. Listen, in two weeks Pepper's going to hold its annual picnic and dance. Will you be there?" He gave her the date and the time.

She hesitated, then nodded.

"If we still feel the same way, then we'll know," he said, then spun on his heel and walked away.

CHAPTER FOUR

"WHAT CAN I TELL YOU about Texas?" Norah asked Sherry as they sat by the swimming pool in the yard behind her sprawling luxury home. Both three-year-old Jeff and baby Grace were napping, and Norah and Sherry were spending a leisurely afternoon soaking up the sun. "Texas is oil wells, cattle and cotton. It's grassy plains and mountains."

"And desert," Sherry added.

"That, too. Texas is chicken-fried steak, black-eyed peas and hot biscuits and gravy. Actually, I've discovered," Norah added with a grin, "that most Texans will eat just about anything. They've downed so many chili peppers over the years that they've burned out their taste buds."

"I've really come to love this state," Sherry admitted, sipping from her glass of iced tea. "Everyone's so friendly."

"It's not only known as the Lone Star state, but a lot of folks call it the Friendship state."

That didn't surprise Sherry.

"The men are hilarious," Norah continued, her eyes sparkling with silent laughter. "Oh, they don't mean to be, but I swear they've got some of the craziest ideas about...well, just about everything. To give you an example, they have this unwritten code, something that has to do with *real* Texans versus everyone else in the world. A real Texan would or wouldn't do any number of things.''

''Such as?''

''Well, a real Texan believes strongly in law and order, except when the law insists upon a fifty-five-mile-an-hour speed limit. They consider that downright unreasonable. Clothes are something else. A real Texan wouldn't dream of decorating his Stetson with feathers or anything, with the possible exception of a snake band, but only if he'd killed the snake and tanned the skin himself. And the jeans! I swear they refuse to wash them until they can stand up on their own.''

Sherry laughed. She'd run into a few of those types herself on her journey across the vast state. But no one could compete with the characters she'd met in Pepper. Mayor Bowie, Donna Jo and Billy Bob. The way that man had manipulated her into remaining in town!

And Cody Bailman kept drifting into her mind, although she'd made numerous attempts to keep him away. Especially the thought of their last meeting, when he'd kissed her in broad daylight in front of half the town. But nothing helped. No matter how hard she tried, Cody Bailman was in her head day and night. It didn't seem possible for a man she'd known for so short a while.

''Sherry.''

Sherry looked up and realized Norah was waving a hand in front of her face. ''You're in another world.''

''Sorry, I was just thinking about, uh, the folks back in Pepper.''

"More than likely it's that cattleman you were telling me about."

Sherry lowered her gaze again, not surprised Norah had read her so easily. "I can't stop thinking about him. I thought that once I was with you I'd be able to get some perspective on what happened between us. Not that anything really did—happen, I mean. Good heavens, I was only in town a little more than twenty-four hours."

"You like him, don't you?"

"That's just it," Sherry said, reaching for her drink and gripping it tightly. "I don't know how I feel about him. It's all messed up in my mind. I don't know Cody well enough to form an opinion, and yet..."

"And yet, you find yourself thinking about him, wishing you could be with him and missing him. All this seems impossible because until a few days ago he wasn't even in your life."

"Yes," Sherry returned emphatically, amazed at the way Norah could clarify her thoughts. "That's exactly what I'm feeling."

"I thought so." Norah relaxed against the cushion on the patio chair and sighed softly, lifting her face to the sun. "It was that way with me after Rowdy was released from the hospital and went home to Texas. My life felt so empty without him. It was like a giant hole had opened up inside me.... He'd only been in the hospital a couple of weeks, but it already seemed as if my whole world revolved around him."

"Rowdy, fortunately, felt the same way about you," Sherry said, knowing Cody was as perplexed as she was by the attraction *they* shared.

"Not at first," Norah countered. "I amused him, and being stuck in traction the way he was, the poor guy was desperate for some comic relief. I happened to be handy. Being Valerie's sister lent to my appeal, too. You know, he actually came to Orchard Valley to break up her engagement to Colby! I don't think it was until much later that he fell in love with me—later than he's willing to admit now, at any rate."

"Don't be so sure." Sherry still remembered the chaos Rowdy Cassidy had brought into the tidy world of Orchard Valley General. His plane had crashed in a nearby field and he'd been taken, seriously injured, to Emergency. He'd been a terrible patient—demanding and cantankerous. Only one nurse could handle him.... Sherry had known he was in love with Norah long before he ever left the hospital, even if he wasn't aware of it himself. Norah's feelings had been equally clear to her. It seemed she could judge another's emotions better than her own.

"I'm rather sorry you took this position in Pepper," Norah said softly. "I know it's pure selfishness on my part, but I was hoping if you moved to Texas you'd settle closer to Houston."

"I don't think I realized how large this state is. Central Texas didn't look that far from Houston on the map. I found out differently when I had to drive it."

"I wish you'd taken the time to stop in San Antonio. Rowdy took me there for our first anniversary, and we fell in love all over again. Of course, it might have had something to do with the flagstone walks, the marvelous boutiques and the outdoor cafés." Norah sighed longingly with the memory. "The air was scented by jasmine. If I close my eyes I can almost smell it now.''

Norah's face grew wistful.

"We rode in a river taxi down the San Antonio River and...oh, I swear it was the most romantic weekend we've ever spent together."

"I'll make a point of visiting San Antonio soon," Sherry said.

"Don't go alone," Norah insisted. "It's a place meant for lovers."

"Okay. I'll make sure I'm crazy in love before I make any traveling plans."

"Good." Norah was satisfied.

Rowdy returned home from the office earlier than usual with wonderful news. He and Norah were hoping to adopt two small children who'd been orphaned the year before. Because of some legal difficulties, the adoption had been held up in the courts.

"It looks like we're going to be adding to our family shortly," Rowdy explained, kissing Norah's cheek before claiming the chair next to her and reaching for her hand.

It was almost painful for Sherry to see these two people so deeply in love. It reminded her how very alone she was, how very isolated her life had become as more and more of her friends found their life's partner. Sherry felt like someone on the outside looking in.

"Grace's new tooth broke through this afternoon," Norah told Rowdy after she poured him a glass of iced tea and added a slice of lemon.

"This I've got to see," he said, heading toward the house.

"Rowdy," Norah called after him. "Let her sleep. She was fussy most of the afternoon."

"I thought I'd take her and Jeff swimming."

"You can, but wait till they wake up from their naps." Norah looked to Sherry and sighed softly. "I swear Rowdy's nothing more than a big kid himself. He's looking for someone to play with."

"He's wonderful. I could almost be jealous."

"There's no need," Norah said, reaching over and squeezing Sherry's arm. "Your turn's coming, and I think it's going to be sooner than you expect."

"I hope so," Sherry said, but she didn't have any faith in her friend's assessment.

"Sherry," Rowdy said, turning back from the house. "I did a bit of checking on that cattleman you mentioned the other night." He removed a slip of paper from his inside pocket. "Cody James Bailman," he read, "born thirty-five years ago, married at twenty-one, widowed, one daughter named Heather. Owns a ten-thousand-acre spread outside of Pepper. He was elected president of the local Cattlemen's Association three years running."

"That's it?" Norah pressed.

"He raises quarter horses, as well as cattle."

That didn't tell Sherry much more than she already knew.

"He seems decent enough. I spoke to a man who's known Bailman for several years and he thinks real highly of him. If you want my advice, I say marry the fellow, present him with a couple of kids in the next few years and see what happens."

"Rowdy!" Norah chastised.

"That's what you did to me, and everything worked out, didn't it?"

"Circumstances are just a tad different, dear," Norah said, glancing apologetically toward Sherry.

"Marriage would do them both good," Rowdy continued. He looked at Sherry and nodded as if the decision had already been made. "Marry the man."

"MARRY THE MAN." As Sherry drove toward Pepper several days later, Rowdy's words clung to her mind. Cody's parting words returned to haunt her, as well. *Then we'll know.* But what could they possibly have learned from their two weeks apart? Sherry hadn't a clue.

Because of a flat tire fifty miles on the other side of nowhere, followed by a long delay at the service station, Sherry was much later than she'd hoped. In fact, she was going to miss a portion of the scheduled festivities, including the parade. But with any luck she'd be in town before the dance started.

She'd tried phoning Cody's ranch from the service station, but there hadn't been any answer. No doubt everyone was enjoying the community celebration. With nothing left to do, she drove on, not stopping for lunch, until she arrived in Pepper.

The town had put on its best dress for this community event. A banner stretched across Main Street, declaring Pepper Days. The lampposts were decorated with a profusion of blue bonnets, and red, white and blue crepe paper was strung from post to post.

Several brightly painted cardboard signs directed her toward the city park and the barbecue. As soon as she turned off Main and onto Spruce, Sherry was assailed by the scent of mesquite and roasting beef. Several signs directed participants and onlookers to the far side of the park where a chili cook-off was in progress. Sherry was fortunate to find a parking space on a side street. Country-and-western music blared from loudspeakers, and colorful Chinese lanterns dotted the cottonwood trees.

People were milling around the park, and Sherry didn't recognize anyone. She would have liked to freshen up before meeting Cody, but she was already late and didn't want to take the time. Besides, her calf-length denim skirt, cowboy boots and Western shirt with a white leather fringe were perfect for the festivities. The skirt and shirt had been a welcome-to-Texas gift from Norah.

"Sherry!"

She twirled around to see Cody's daughter waving and racing toward her. Not quite prepared for the impact as Heather flung herself at her, throwing her arms around her waist and squeezing tightly, Sherry nearly toppled backwards but caught herself just in time.

"I knew you'd come! I never doubted, not even for a second. Have you seen my dad yet?"

"No, I just arrived."

"He didn't think you were going to come. Men are like that, you know. It's all a way to keep from being disappointed, don't you think?"

But Cody's attitude disappointed Sherry. "I said I'd be here."

"I know, but Dad didn't have a lot of faith that you'd show. I did, though. What do you think of my hair?" Heather looked extremely pretty with her thick dark hair loose and curling down her back. She whipped back the curls and tossed her head as if she were doing a shampoo commercial. She looked up at Sherry, her eyes wide and guileless, as though she'd practiced the look countless times in front of the bathroom mirror. "Come on, let's go find my father before he pines away."

It didn't take long for Sherry to spot Cody. He was talking to a group of men who were gathered in a circle. Their discussion appeared to be a heated one, and Sherry guessed the topic was politics. It wasn't until she was closer that she realized they were contesting the pros and cons of adding jalapeño peppers to Billy Bob's barbecue sauce.

"They're just neighbors," Heather whispered as they approached. "Dad can talk to them anytime."

Unwilling to interrupt him, Sherry stopped the girl's progress.

"But this could go on for hours!" Heather protested, apparently loud enough for her father to hear, because at that moment he turned and saw them.

His eyes moved from his daughter to Sherry, and he looked as if he couldn't believe she was really there. He excused himself to his friends and began walking toward her.

"Hello, Cody." The words seemed to stick like tar in Sherry's throat.

"I didn't think you were going to come," he said.

"I had a flat tire on the way, and it took ages to repair. I phoned, but I guess everyone at the Lucky Horseshoe had already left for the picnic."

"Are you hungry?"

"Starved," she admitted.

Cody pulled a wad of bills from his pocket, peeled off several ones and handed them to Heather. "Bring Sherry a plate of the barbecue beef."

"But, Dad, I wanted to talk to her and—"

Cody silenced the protest with a single look.

"All right, I get the picture. You want to be alone with her. How long do you want me to stay away?" The question was posed with an elaborate sigh. "An hour? Two?"

"We'll be under the willow tree," Cody said, ignoring her questions and pointing to an enormous weeping willow about fifty feet away.

"The willow tree," Heather repeated, her voice dipping suggestively. "Good choice, Dad. Real good. I couldn't have thought of a better place myself."

Cody gave a sigh of relief as Heather trotted off. "You'll have to forgive my daughter," he said shaking his head. Then he smiled. "She was as eager for you to return as I was."

His words and smile went a long way toward reassuring Sherry. Their separation had felt like a lifetime to her. Two weeks away from a man she'd known only briefly; it didn't make sense, but then, little did any longer.

All at once Sherry felt scared. Scared of all the feelings that were crowding up inside her. Scared of being with Cody again, of kissing him again, of making more of this attraction than he intended or wanted. Her feelings were powerful, alien. At first she attributed them to being with Norah and Rowdy and seeing how happy they were.

Now here she was with Cody, sitting under the shadowy arms of a weeping willow, and her confusion returned a hundredfold. This man touched her in a thousand indescribable ways, but she was troubled; she wasn't sure her feelings were because of Cody himself. Maybe it was the warm promise he represented. The happiness waiting for her just around the corner, out of reach. She desperately wanted the joy her friends had found. She was tired of being alone. Tired of walking into an empty apartment. Tired of being a bridesmaid, instead of bride. She wanted a husband, a home and a family. Was that so much to ask?

Cody spread out a blanket for them to sit on. "How were your friends?"

"Very much in love." It wasn't what Sherry had meant to say, but the first thing that sprang to her lips. She looked away embarrassed.

"Newlyweds?"

She shook her head. "They've been married four years and have two children. Within a few weeks they'll be adding two adopted ones to the family."

"They sound like a compassionate, generous couple."

His words warmed her heart like a July sun. Rowdy and Norah *were* two of the most generous people Sherry had ever known. It was as if they were so secure in their love for each other that it spilled over and flowed out to those around them.

"What's wrong?"

This man seemed to read her so accurately that nothing less than the truth would do. "I'm scared to death of seeing you again, of feeling the things I do for you. I don't even know you, and I feel . . . That's just it, I don't know what I feel."

He laughed. "You're not alone. I keep telling myself this whole thing is nuttier than a pecan grove. I don't really know you, either. Why you, out of all the women I've met over the years?"

"I'm not interrupting anything, am I?" Heather burst through the hanging branches and stepped onto the blanket. She crossed her legs and slowly lowered herself on the ground before handing Sherry a plate heaped high with potato salad, barbecued chicken and one of the biggest dill pickles Sherry had ever seen.

Heather licked her fingertips clean. "They've run out of beef. I told Mayor Bowie this was for Sherry, and he wanted me to ask you to save a dance for him. He's been cooking all afternoon, and he says he's looking forward to seeing a pretty face, instead of a pot of Billy Bob's barbecue sauce."

"This smells heavenly," Sherry said, taking the plate and digging in.

Cody looked pointedly at his daughter, expecting her to make herself scarce, but she looked just as pointedly back. "So, have you come to any conclusions?" Heather asked.

"No. But then we haven't had much time *alone,* have we?"

"You've had enough."

Cody closed his eyes. "Heather, please."

"Are you going to ask Sherry to dance, or are you going to wait for Mayor Bowie to steal her away from you? Dad, you can't be so nonchalant about this courting business. Aren't you the one who insists the early bird catches the worm? You know Mayor Bowie's fond of Sherry."

"The mayor's a married man."

"So?" Heather said, seeming to enjoy their exchange. "That didn't stop Russell Forester from running off with Milly You-know-who."

If the color in his neck was any indication, Cody's frustration level was quickly reaching its peak. But Sherry welcomed the intrusion. She needed space and time to sort through her feelings. Everything had become so intense so quickly. If Heather hadn't interrupted them when she had, Sherry was certain she'd have been in Cody's arms. It was too soon to cloud their feelings with sexual awareness.

"The chicken was delicious," Sherry said, licking her fingers clean of the spicy sauce. "I can't remember ever tasting any better."

"Cody Bailman, are you hiding Sherry under that tree with you?" The toes of a pair of snakeskin boots stepped on the outer edges of the blanket just under the tree's protective foliage.

Heather cast her father a righteous look and whispered heatedly, "I *told* you Mayor Bowie was going to ask her to dance first."

Cody stood and parted the willow's hanging branches. "She's eating."

"Howdy, Mayor," Sherry said, looking up at him, a chicken leg poised in front of her mouth. "I understand you're the chef responsible for this feed. You can cook for me anytime."

"I'm not a bad dancer, either. I thought I'd see if you wouldn't mind taking a spin with an old coot like me."

She laughed. "You're not so old."

"What'll your wife think?" Cody asked, his tone jocular, but with an underlying...what? Annoyance? Jealousy? Sherry wasn't sure.

Pepper's mayor waved his hand dismissively. "Hazel won't care. Good grief, I've been married to the woman for thirty-seven years. Besides, she's talking to her friends, and you know how that bunch loves to idle away an afternoon gossiping. I thought I'd give them something to talk about."

"Sherry?" Cody glanced at her as if he expected her to decline.

Frankly, Sherry was flattered to have two men vying for her attention, even if one of them was old enough to be her father and looked as if he'd sampled a bit too much of his own cooking over the years.

"Why, Mayor, I'd be delighted."

Cody didn't look at all pleased.

"I told you something like this was going to happen," Heather reminded him indignantly. "Your problem, Dad, is that you never listen to me. I read romance novels, I know about these things."

A laugh hovered on Sherry's lips. She hoisted herself up and accepted Mayor Bowie's hand as he led her to the dancing platform.

Cody and Heather followed close behind. Because Mayor Bowie was chatting, she couldn't quite make out the conversation going on between father and daughter, but it seemed to her Heather was still chastising her father for his tardiness.

Although it was still early evening, the dance floor was already crowded. Willie Nelson was crooning a melodic ballad as the mayor deftly escorted Sherry onto the large black-and-white-checkered platform.

He tucked his hand at her waist and stretched her arm out to one side, then smoothly led her across the floor.

"How're you doin', Sherry?" Said a woman's voice.

She turned to see Donna Jo dancing with the sheriff. Sherry waved with her free hand. Doc Lindsey danced by with Mrs. Colson, first in one direction and then another in what looked like a crazy version of a tango.

Mayor Bowie was surprisingly light on his feet, and he whirled Sherry around so many times she started to get dizzy. When the dance ended, she looked up to find Cody standing next to the mayor.

"I believe this dance is mine," he said.

"Of course." The mayor gracefully stepped aside and turned to Heather. Tucking his arm around his middle, he bowed and asked the giggling twelve-year-old for the pleasure of the next dance.

Heather cast Sherry a proud look and responded with a dignified curtsy.

"So, we meet again," Sherry said, slipping her left arm onto Cody's shoulder.

"You should have danced with me first," he muttered.

"Why?" She wasn't sure she approved of his tone or his attitude. Mayor Bowie certainly couldn't be seen as competition!

"If you had, you'd have saved me a lecture from my daughter. She seems to have been doing research on romance, and apparently I've committed several blunders. According to Heather, my tactics aren't the way to ensnare today's sophisticated woman." He made a wry grimace.

Sherry couldn't help but notice they were doing little more than shuffling their feet, while other couples whirled around them. Cody seemed to notice the same thing and he exhaled sharply.

"That's another thing." he said. "My own daughter suggested I take dancing lessons." He snorted. "Me, as if I have the time for that kind of nonsense. Listen, if you want to date a man who's light on his feet, you better know right now I'm no Fred Astaire and never will be."

Actually Sherry had figured that out for herself, not that it mattered. Cody sighed again.

"Is something else troubling you?" Sherry asked.

"Yes," he admitted grudgingly. "You feel damn good in my arms. I'm probably breaking some romance code by telling you that. Damned if I know what a man's supposed to say and what he isn't."

Sherry pressed the side of her head to his chin and closed her eyes. "That was very sweet."

Cody was silent for the next few moments. "What about you?" he asked gruffly.

Sherry pulled back enough for him to read the question in her eyes. His own were dark and troubled.

"It'd help matters if you told me the same thing," he said. "That you...like being with me, too." He shook his head. "I've got to tell you, I'm feeling real silly."

"I do enjoy being with you."

He didn't seem to hear. "I feel like a pinned and mounted Monarch butterfly on display for everyone to inspect."

"Why's that?"

He looked away, but not before she read his frown. "Let me just say that kissing you in public didn't help matters any. It was the most ridiculous thing I've done in my thirty-four years. I made a damn fool of myself in front of the entire town."

"I wouldn't say that," she whispered, close to his ear. "I liked it."

"That's the problem." He grunted. "So did I. You know what I think? This is all Heather's doing. It started with that crazy project of hers. I swear that kid is going to ruin me yet."

"Heather's project?"

"Forget I said that."

"Why are you so angry? Is it because I danced with the mayor?"

"Good heavens, no. This has nothing to do with that."

"Then what *does* it have to do with?"

"You," he grumbled.

Dolly Parton's tremulous tones were coming out of the speakers now. It was a fast-paced number, not that Cody noticed. He didn't alter his footwork, but continued his laborious two-step.

"Cody, maybe we'd better sit down."

"We can't."

"Why not?" she asked.

"Because the minute we do, someone else is sure to ask you to dance, and I can't allow that."

She stared up at him, growing more confused by the moment. "Why not? Cody, you're being ridiculous."

"I don't need you to tell me that. I've been ridiculous ever since I saw you holding Ellie's baby in your arms. I've been behaving like a lovesick calf from the first moment I kissed you. I can understand what caused a normally sane, sensible man like Luke Johnson to chase after a sports car with his horse because he couldn't stand to let the woman he loved leave town. And dammit, I don't like it. Not one bit.''

What had first sounded rather romantic was fast losing its appeal. ''I don't like what I feel for you, either, Cody Bailman. I had a perfectly good life until you barged in.''

''So did I!''

''I think we should end this whole thing,'' she said, pulling away from him. ''Before we say something we'll regret.'' She dropped her arms to her sides and stared up at him.

''Great,'' he muttered. ''Let's just do that.''

With so many couples whirling about, Sherry found it difficult to make her way off the dance floor, but she managed, sidestepping her way. To her consternation, Cody followed close behind her.

Spotting Ellie sitting beneath the shade of an oak tree, Sherry headed in that direction, determined to ignore Cody. She was halfway across the park when she heard him call out after her.

''Sherry! Dammit, woman, wait up for me!''

She didn't bother to turn around to see what had detained him. When she reached Ellie, the woman smiled brightly up at her.

''I see you've just tangled with the most stubborn man this side of Luke Johnson.''

CHAPTER FIVE

"CODY INFURIATES ME," Sherry announced, plopping herself next to Ellie Johnson on the blanket under the tree. She wrapped her arms around her knees and exhaled sharply in frustration.

"Men have infuriated women since the dawn of time. They're totally irrational beings," Ellie said calmly while gently patting her infant son's back. Philip was sleeping contentedly against her shoulder.

"Irrational isn't the word for it. They're insane."

"That, too," Ellie agreed readily.

"No one else but Cody could use a compliment to insult someone!"

"Luke did when we first started dating," Ellie told her. "He'd say things like 'You're not bad-looking for a skinny girl.'"

Despite her annoyance with Cody, Sherry laughed.

Cody had been waylaid by Luke, Sherry noticed. Luke carried Christina Lynn on his shoulders, and the toddler's arms were reaching toward the sky in an effort to touch the fluffy clouds. Sherry hoped Ellie's husband was giving Cody a few pointers about relationships.

Forcing her thoughts away from the cattleman, Sherry sighed and watched Ellie with her baby son. Philip had awoken and she turned him in her arms, situated a receiving blanket over her shoulder, then bared her breast.

"He's thriving," Ellie said happily. "I can't thank you enough for being with me the night he was born. Having you there made all the difference in the world."

"It wasn't me doing all the work," Sherry reminded her.

"Then let's just say we make an excellent team." Ellie stroked her son's face with her index finger as he sucked greedily at her breast. "I'm really pleased you're going to live in Pepper. I feel like you're a friend already."

Sherry glanced up to discover Heather marching her way, hands on hips. Her eyes were indignant as she stopped and briefly talked to her father and Luke before tossing her hands in the air and striding over to Ellie and Sherry.

"What did he do now?" Cody's daughter demanded. "He said something stupid, right?" In a display of complete disgust, she slapped her hands against her sides and lowered herself to the blanket next to Sherry. "I tried to coach him, but a lot of good that did." She eyed her father angrily. "No wonder he's never remarried. The man obviously needs more help than me and romance novels can offer him."

Ellie and Sherry shared a smile. "Don't try so hard, Heather."

"But I want Dad to remarry so I can have a baby brother or sister. Or one of each."

"Heather," Sherry said, "your father said something about a project you were involved in, and then he immediately seemed to regret mentioning it."

"He's never going to let me forget it, either," the girl muttered. "Neither is anyone else in this town."

"You have to admit, it was rather amusing," Ellie added.

"Oh, sure, everyone got a big laugh out of it—at my expense, too."

"Out of what?" Sherry wanted to know.

"My 4-H project. I've been a member for several years and each spring we work on a single project for the following twelve months. One year I raised rabbits, and another I worked with my horse, Misty. This spring I gave the whole town a big laugh when I decided I wanted my project to be helping my dad find himself a wife."

"You weren't serious!" Sherry was mortified.

"I was at the time, but now I can see it was all pretty silly," Heather continued. "Anyway, everyone talked about it for days. That's one of the worst things about living in a small town. Dad was furious with me, which didn't help."

Sherry wasn't sure what to think. "That's why you were so excited when you met me."

"You're darn right, especially when I found you sleeping in Dad's bed."

Sherry shot a glance at Ellie and felt her face grow warm. "Cody slept in the guest room."

"My friend, Carrie Whistler, spent the night before with me, and I was supposed to have changed the sheets, but I forgot," Heather explained further to Ellie, then turned her attention back to Sherry. "You're just perfect for Dad, and I was hoping you might grow to, you know, love him. I think you'd make a terrific mother."

Sherry felt tears burn the back of her eyes. "I don't know when anyone's paid me a higher compliment, Heather, but love doesn't work that way. I'm sorry. I can't marry your father just because you want a baby brother and sister."

"But you like him, don't you?"

"Yes, but—"

"Until he said something stupid and ruined everything." Heather's face tightened.

"Why don't you let those two work matters out for themselves?" Ellie suggested to the girl. "Your interference will only cause problems."

"But Dad won't get anything right without me!"

"He married your mother, didn't he?" Ellie reminded her. "It seems to me he'll do perfectly fine all on his own."

"I *like* Sherry, though. Better than anyone, and Dad does, too. His problem is he thinks love's a big waste of time. He told me he wanted to cut to the chase and be done with it."

"He said that?" Sherry glared over at him. Cody must have sensed it, because he glanced her way and grimaced at the intensity of her look. He said something to Luke, who turned their way, also. Luke's shoulders lifted in a shrug. Then he patted Cody's back and the two of them headed in the direction of the cook-off area.

"He said he's too busy with the ranch to date anyone."

"I'm sure that's true," Sherry said. She felt like a complete fool for having constructed this wild romantic fantasy in her mind. Cody had never been interested in her. From the very first, he'd been looking to mollify his daughter. She just happened upon the scene at a convenient moment. Sherry felt sick to her stomach. This was what happened when she allowed herself to believe in romance, to believe in love. It seemed all so easy for her friends, but it wasn't for her.

"I've had a long day," Sherry said, suddenly feeling weary. "I think I'll go unpack my bags, soak in the tub and make an early night of it."

"You can't!" Heather protested. "I signed you and Dad up for the three-legged race, the egg toss and the water-balloon toss. They have the races in the evening because it's too hot in the afternoon."

"I don't think your father's interested in having me as a partner."

"But he is," Heather insisted. "He's won the egg toss for years and years, and it's really important to him. It's one of those ego things."

"Unfortunately, he's already got egg on his face," Sherry muttered to Ellie who laughed outright.

"Please stay," Heather pleaded. "Please, please, please. If you don't, I can't see myself ever forgiving Dad for ruining this golden opportunity."

Sherry was beginning to understand Cody's frustration with his daughter. "Heather, don't play matchmaker. It'll do more harm than good. If your father is genuinely interested in dating me, he'll do so without you goading him into it. Promise me you'll stay out of this."

Heather looked at the ground and her pretty blue eyes grew sad. "It's just that I like you so much and we could have so much fun together."

"We certainly don't need your father for that."

"We don't?"

"Trust me," Ellie inserted, "a man would only get in the way."

"Would you go school-clothes shopping with me? I mean, to a real town with a mall with more than three stores, and spend the day with me?"

"I'd love it."

Heather lowered her gaze again, then murmured. "I need help with bras and...and other stuff."

Sherry smiled. "We'll drive into Abilene and make it a day."

Heather's eyes lit up like sparklers on the Fourth of July. "That'd be great!"

"So, I'll leave you to partner your dad on the egg toss."

The glimmer in her eyes didn't fade. "I was thinking the same thing." She looked mischievous. "This could well be the year Dad loses his title as the egg champion."

"Heather," Sherry chastised, "be nice to your father."

"Oh, I will," she promised, "especially since you and I have reached an understanding."

"Good. Then I'm heading over to the clinic now."

"You're sure you won't stay? There's a fireworks display scheduled for tonight. It's even better than the one we had on the Fourth."

"I think Sherry's seen all the fireworks she wants for one night," Ellie put in.

"You're right, I have. We'll talk later, Heather. Goodbye, Ellie." She leaned over and kissed the top of Philip's head. "Let's make a point of getting together soon."

"I'd like that," Ellie said.

Sherry was halfway back to her car when Cody caught up with her. He fell into step with her. "I didn't mean to offend you." He said after a moment.

Sherry sighed and briefly closed her eyes. "I know."

"But you're still mad?"

"No, discouraged perhaps, but not mad." She reached her car and unlocked it. "I talked to Heather and she told me about her 4-H project. It explained a lot."

"Like what?"

"Like why you're interested in me. Why you chose to drive me to the ranch, instead of town after Ellie's baby was born."

"That had nothing to do with it. We were both dog-tired, and my place was a lot closer than town."

"You don't need to worry," Sherry said, not the least bit interested in getting into another debate with him. She was truly weary and not in the best of moods, fighting the heat, disappointment and the effects of an undernourished romantic heart. "I had a nice chat with Heather. You've done a wonderful job raising her, Cody. She's a delightful girl. Unless you object, I'd like to be her friend. She and I already made plans to go clothes shopping in Abilene."

"Of course I don't object."

"Thank you." She slipped inside her car and started the engine. She would have driven away, but Cody prevented her from closing the door.

He scratched his temple and frowned darkly. "I don't mean to be obtuse, but what does all this mean?"

"Nothing, really. I'm just cutting to the chase," she said, "and explaining that it isn't necessary for you to play out this charade any longer."

"What charade?"

"Of being attracted to me."

"I *am* attracted to you."

"But you wish you weren't."

He opened and closed his mouth twice before he answered. "I should have known you'd throw that back in my face. You're right. I don't have time for courtin' and the like. I've got a ranch to run, and this is one of the busiest times of the year."

Sherry blinked, not sure what to make of Cody. He seemed sincere about not meaning to offend her, and yet he constantly said and did things that infuriated her.

"The problem is," Cody continued, still frowning, "if I don't stake my claim on you now, there'll be ten other ranchers all vying for your attention."

"Stake your claim?" He made her sound like an acre of water-rich land.

"You know," he said. "Let everyone in town see you're my woman."

"I'm not *any* man's woman."

"Not yet, but I'd like you to think about being mine." He removed his hat; Sherry guessed that meant he intended her to take him seriously. "If you'd be willing to run off and get married, then—"

"Then *what*?"

"Then we'd be done with it. See, I don't have the time or energy to waste on courtin' a woman."

Sherry nodded slowly, all the while chewing on the inside of her cheek to keep from saying something she'd regret. So much for romance! So much for sipping champagne and feeding each other chocolate-covered strawberries in the moonlight, a fantasy Sherry had carried with her for years. Or a romantic weekend in San Antonio, the way Norah had described. No wonder Heather was frustrated with her father. The girl must feel as if she was butting her head against a brick wall.

"Well?" Cody demanded.

Sherry stared at him for several moments. "You aren't serious, are you?"

"I'm dead serious. I like you. You like me. What else is there? Sure we can spend the next several months going through the ridiculous rituals society places on couples, or we can use the common sense God gave us and be done with this romance nonsense."

"And do what?" Sherry asked innocently.

"Marry, of course. I haven't stopped thinking about you in two weeks. You didn't stop thinking about me, either. I saw it in your eyes no more'n an hour ago. You know what it's like when we kiss. Instead of playing games with each other, why not admit you want me as much as I want you? I never did understand why women need to complicate a basic human need with a bunch of flowery words. If you want kids, all the better. I certainly won't object."

Sherry carefully composed her response. Apparently she took longer than he thought necessary.

"Well?" he pressed.

She looked up at him, her gaze deliberately calm. "I'd rather eat fried rattlesnake than marry a man who proposed to me the way you just did."

Cody stared at her as if not sure what to make of her response, then slammed his hat back on his head. "This is the problem with you women. You want everything served to you on a silver platter. For your information, fried rattlesnake happens to be pretty good. Doesn't taste all that much different from chicken."

"Well, I wouldn't eat it even if it *was* served on a silver platter." Sherry snapped. This conversation was over. He'd only frustrated her before, but now she was really angry.

"That's your decision, then?"

"That's my decision," she said tightly.

"You're rejecting my proposal?"

"Yup."

"I should have figured as much," Cody said. "I knew even before I opened my mouth that you were going to be pigheaded about this."

"Don't feel bad," she said with feigned amiability. "I'm sure there're plenty of women who'd leap at your offer. I just don't happen to be one of them." She reached for the handle of the still-open door, and he was obliged to move out of the way.

"Good night, Cody."

"Goodbye," he muttered, and stalked away. He turned back once as if he wanted to argue with her some more, but apparently changed his mind. Sherry threw the GEO into gear and drove off.

"WHAT HAPPENED between my dad and you after we talked?" Heather asked in a whisper over the telephone. She'd called Sherry first thing the following morning.

"Heather, I'm on duty. I can't talk now."

"Who's sick?"

"No one at the moment, but—"

"If there's no one there, then it won't hurt to talk to me for just a couple of minutes, will it? Please?"

"Nothing happened between your dad and me." Which of course wasn't true. She'd been proposed to, if you could call it that, for the first time in her life.

"Then why is Dad acting like a wounded bear? Janey threatened to quit this morning, and she's been working for Dad since before I was born."

"Why don't you ask your father?"

"You're kidding, right? No one wants to talk to him. Even Slim's staying out of his way."

"Give him time. He'll cool down."

"If I was willing to wait, I wouldn't be calling you."

"Heather," Sherry said, growing impatient, "this is between your father and me. Let's just leave it at that, all right?"

"You don't want my help?"

"No," Sherry returned emphatically, "I don't. Please, leave this to us to settle."

"All right," the girl agreed reluctantly. "I'll drop whatever it is that *didn't* happen that you don't want to talk about."

"Thank you."

"I hope you realize what a sacrifice this is."

"Oh, I do."

"You might think that just because I'm a kid I don't know certain things. But I know more than either you or Dad realize. I—"

Sherry rolled her eyes. "I need to get off the phone."

Heather released a great gusty sigh. "All right. We're still going shopping for school clothes, aren't we? Soon, too, because school starts in less than two weeks."

"You bet." Sherry suggested a day and a time and reminded Heather to check with her father. "I'll make reservations at a nice hotel, and we'll spend the night."

"That'll be great! Oh, Sherry, I really wish you and Dad could get along, because I think you're fabulous."

"I think you're pretty fabulous yourself, honey. Now listen, I must go. I can't tie up the line."

"I understand. Next time I call, I'll have Mrs. Colson take a message. You can call me back later when you're not on duty."

"That sounds perfect."

SHERRY HAD JUST FINISHED with her first patient of the afternoon, a four-year-old with a bad ear infection, when Mrs. Colson handed her a telephone message. Sherry should have suspected something wasn't right when the receptionist smiled so broadly.

Sherry took the slip and stuck it into the pocket of her white uniform jacket, waiting until she was alone to read it. When she did, she sank into a chair and closed her eyes. The call was from Heather. She'd talked to her father, and he apparently had business in Abilene that same weekend and was making arrangements for the three of them to travel together.

This was going to be difficult. Knowing Cody, he'd turn a simple shopping trip into a test of her patience and endurance. She'd have to set some ground rules.

CODY WAS SCHEDULED to pick her up at the clinic early Saturday morning, and she was standing on the porch waiting for him. It'd been a week since she'd last seen him, four days since their stilted conversation on the phone—and a lifetime since she'd dreaded any trip more.

Her heart sank to the deepest pit of her stomach when the white Cadillac pulled to a stop in front of the clinic's porch, where she was waiting.

Cody got out of the car and climbed the steps. Sherry saw Heather scramble over the front seat and into the back.

"Hello," Sherry said, her grip on her overnight case punishing.

"Hello." His voice was devoid of emotion as he reached for her bag.

"I thought we should talk before we leave," she said when he was halfway back down the steps.

"All right." He didn't sound eager.

"Let's call a truce. It shouldn't be difficult to be civil to one another, should it? There isn't any reason for us to discuss our differences now or ever again, for that matter."

"No," he agreed, "it shouldn't be the least bit difficult to be civil."

And surprisingly, it wasn't. The radio filled in silence during the long drive, and when the stations faded, Heather bubbled over with eager chatter. Cody seemed to go out of his way to be amiable, and Sherry found her reserve melting as the miles slipped past.

The hotel Cody chose in Abilene was situated close to a large shopping mall. Heather was ready to head for the shops the minute they checked into their spacious two-bedroom suite.

"Hold your horses," Cody insisted. He had his briefcase with him. "I probably won't be back until later this evening."

"What about dinner?" Heather wanted to know. "I've got an appointment."

"Don't worry about us," Sherry told him. "Either we'll order something from room service or eat downstairs. If we're feeling adventurous, we'll go out, but I don't imagine we'll go far."

"What time will you be back, Dad?"

Cody paused. "I can't say. I could be late, so don't wait up for me."

"Can I watch a movie?" She stood in front of the color television and read over the listings offered on the printed card.

"If Sherry doesn't object, I can't see any reason why not."

Heather hugged her father and he kissed the crown of her head. "Have fun, you two."

"We will," Sherry said.

"Spend your money wisely," he advised on his way out the door, but the look he cast Sherry assured her he trusted her to guide Heather in making the proper selections.

The girl waited until her father was out of the room before she hurled herself onto the beige sofa and carelessly tossed out both arms. "Isn't this great? You brought your swimsuit, didn't you? I did."

Sherry had, but she wasn't sure there'd be enough time for them to use the large hotel pool.

"It's almost as if we were a real family."

"Heather..."

"I know, I know," she said dejectedly, "Dad already lectured me about this. I'm not supposed to say anything that would in any way insin...insinuate that the two of you share any romantic interest in each other." She said this last bit in a voice that sounded as if it were coming from a robot.

"At least your father and I understand one another."

"That's just it. You don't. He really likes you, Sherry. A lot. He'd never admit it, though." She sighed and cocked her head. "Men have a problem with pride, don't they?"

"Women do, too," Sherry said, reaching for her purse. "Are you ready to shop till we drop, or do you want to discuss the troublesome quirks of the male psyche?"

It didn't take Heather more than a second to decide. She bolted from the sofa. "Let's shop!"

Sherry couldn't remember an afternoon she enjoyed more. The mall near the hotel consisted of nearly fifty stores, of which twenty sold clothing, and they made it a matter of pride to visit each and every one. When they were back in the hotel, their arms laden with packages, Sherry discovered they'd bought something in more than half the stores they'd ventured into.

Heather was thrilled with her purchases. She removed the merchandise from the bags and spread the outfits over the twin beds in their room, quickly running out of space. The overflow spilled out onto the sofa and love seat in the living room. Two pairs of crisp jeans and several brightly colored blouses. A couple of jersey pullovers and a lovely soft cardigan. Two bras—the right size for Heather's still-developing figure—and matching panties. Sherry had talked Heather into buying a couple of dresses, too, although the girl insisted the only place she'd ever wear them was to church. Their biggest extravagance had been footwear—five pairs altogether. Boots, sneakers, dress shoes—to go with her Sunday dresses—a sturdy pair for school and a fun pair of bedroom slippers.

Sherry wasn't immune to spending money on herself, and she'd purchased a lovely black crepe evening dress. The top was studded with rhinestone chips that flashed and glittered in the light. Heaven only knew where she was going to wear it, but she'd been unable to resist.

"I have an idea!" Heather announced. "Let's dress up really nice for dinner. I'll wear my dress and new shoes and you can wear *your* new dress, and then we'll go down and order lobster for dinner and charge it to the room so Dad'll pay for it."

An elegant dinner to celebrate their success held a certain appeal—and gave Sherry an unexpected chance to wear her new finery—but charging it to the room didn't seem fair to Cody. "I don't know, Heather..."

"Dad won't mind," Heather assured her. "He's grateful you're willing to shop with me, and he'll be even more pleased now that I have bras that fit me. So, come on—what do you think?"

"I think dinner's a marvelous idea." They could work out the finances later.

"Great." Heather rummaged through the bags stacked on Sherry's bed until she found what she was looking for. "We should do our nails first, though, shouldn't we?"

They'd discovered the hottest shade of pink fingernail polish Sherry had ever seen. Heather had fallen in love with it and convinced Sherry her life wouldn't be complete without it.

"Our hair, too."

"Why not?" If they were going to do themselves up fancy there was no point in half measures. Heather was filled with such boundless enthusiasm Sherry couldn't help being infected with it, too.

Using jasmine-scented bubble bath, Sherry soaked in the tub, washed her hair and piled it high on her head in a white towel. Wrapping herself in a thick terry-cloth robe supplied by the hotel, she rendezvoused with Heather, who'd made use of the second bathroom, back in the living room.

Heather, also wrapped in a thick terry-cloth robe, eagerly set the bottle of hot-pink polish on the table.

"Only for our toes, not our fingers," Sherry instructed.

Heather was clearly disappointed, but she nodded. She balanced one foot then the other against the edge of the coffee table, and Sherry painted her toenails, then had Heather paint hers. They were halfway through this ritual when the key turned in the lock. They both looked up to see Cody stroll casually into the room.

"Dad!" Heather bounded to her feet and raced over to her father. "We had a fabulous day. Wait'll you see what we bought."

Cody set down his briefcase and hugged his daughter. "I take it you had a fun afternoon."

"It was wild. I spent oodles of money. Sherry did, too. She bought this snazzy black dress with diamonds on top, not real ones of course, but they look real. It wasn't on sale, either, but she said she had to have it. When you see her in it, you'll know why."

Cody didn't comment on that. His gaze narrowed when he noticed his daughter's feet. "What have you done to your toes?"

"Isn't it great?" Heather said rhapsodically, wiggling her toes for his inspection.

"Will they make your feet glow in the dark?"

"No, silly!"

Sherry finished painting the last of her own toenails and screwed the top back on the bottle of polish. "We were going to dress up in our new outfits and go downstairs and have dinner in the dining room," she said. "That's all right, isn't it?"

"Anything you want. Dinner's on me."

"Even lobster?" Heather asked, as though she wasn't entirely sure how far his generosity would stretch.

"Even lobster. I just sold off the main part of my herd for the best price I've gotten in years."

"Congratulations." Sherry stood and tightened the cinch of her robe.

"Then you're all through with your business stuff?" Heather asked.

"I'm finished."

"That's even better! You'll join us for dinner, right? You don't mind if Dad comes, do you, Sherry?"

Cody's eyes connected with Sherry's and his smile was slightly cocky, as if to suggest the ball was in her court.

"Of course I don't mind." There wasn't anything else she could say.

"You'll wear your slinky new dress," Heather insisted. "Dad," she turned her attention to her father "—your eyeballs are going to pop out of your head when you see Sherry in it."

Cody's gaze was on his daughter when he spoke. "It's too late for that. They popped out of my head the first minute I saw her."

CHAPTER SIX

SHERRY WASN'T SURE why she felt so nervous. Maybe it had something to do with her new outfit. She had a feeling it was a mistake to wear that particular dress with this particular man.

She arranged her glossy brown hair carefully, piling it on top of her head with dangling wisps at her temples and neck. She wished she could tame her heart just as easily. She tried not to place any credence on this evening out, tried to convince herself it was just a meal between friends. That's all they were. Friends. The promise of more had been wiped away from every-place but her heart. Yet none of her strategies were succeeding. They hadn't even come close to succeeding. She was falling in love with this no-nonsense cattleman, despite the fact there wasn't a romantic bone in his body.

When they'd finished dressing, the three of them met back in the living room. Sherry endured—or was it thrilled to?—Cody's scrutiny. The dress was modest, sleeveless with a dropped waist. The skirt flared out at her hips in a triple layer of sleek ruffles. The high-heeled black sandals were the perfect complement.

"Doesn't Sherry look like a million bucks?" Heather asked.

Without taking his eyes from Sherry, Cody nodded. "Very nice."

"Heather, too," Sherry said.

Cody seemed chagrined that he needed to be reminded to compliment his daughter. His eyes widened with appreciation as he gazed at his daughter.

"Heather," he murmured. "Why...you seem all grown-up."

"I'm nearly thirteen, you know, and that means I'm almost a woman."

"You certainly look like one in that pretty dress." The glance he flashed at Sherry was filled with surprised gratitude. He seemed to be asking how she'd managed to convince his daughter to buy something other than jeans and cowboy boots.

Seeing Cody in a smart sport jacket with a crisp blue shirt and a string tie had a curious effect on Sherry. She couldn't look at him and not be stirred. As much as she hated to admit it, he was a handsome devil. When they'd first met, she'd been struck by the sense of strength and authority she sensed in him. Those same traits were more prominent than ever now.

"Are we going to dinner, or are we going to stand around and stare at each other all evening?" Heather said bluntly, looking from her father to Sherry and then back again.

"By all means, let's eat," Cody put in.

"Yes, let's." Sherry was surprised by how thin and wavery her voice sounded. Apparently she wasn't the only one who noticed, because Heather cast her a curious look, then grinned broadly.

Dinner was an elegant affair. The small dining room was beautifully decorated with antique fixtures and furnishings. The tables were covered with crisp, white linen tablecloths, and the lights were muted. Both Heather and Sherry ordered the lobster-tail dinner while Cody opted for a thick T-bone steak. When a three-piece musical ensemble started to play, Heather glanced at both her father and Sherry.

"You're going to dance, aren't you?" she said.

"The music is more for mood than dancing," Sherry explained, although she wouldn't have objected if Cody had offered. But she knew he didn't much care for dancing, so an offer wasn't likely.

Their salads arrived, all Caesars with big crusty croutons. Heather fairly gobbled hers, and when Sherry looked her way, silently suggesting she eat more slowly, the girl wiped the dressing from the corner of her mouth and shrugged. "I'm too hungry to linger over my food the way you and Dad seem to want to."

Sherry's appetite was almost nil, a stark contrast to an hour earlier—before Cody had returned to the suite. She was almost sorry he was with them, because she couldn't seem to enjoy her food. But although she was uncomfortably aware of his presence, she was still glad to be sharing this time with him and Heather.

Their entrées arrived, and Sherry was grateful to Heather, who singlehandedly carried the dinner conversation. She chattered almost nonstop between bites of lobster, relating the details of the afternoon. Cody concentrated almost entirely on his food, occasionally murmuring a brief response to his daughter's recitations.

But whatever was happening between Cody and her, if indeed anything was, felt strange to Sherry. Cody seemed withdrawn from her both physically and emotionally. A sort of sultry tension filled the air about them, as if they were both waging battles against themselves, against the strong pull of the attraction they shared. Thank goodness, she thought, for Heather's easy banter.

Sherry barely touched her meal, but nothing went to waste, because after Heather downed her own dinner, she polished off what remained of Sherry's.

When their dinner plates had been taken away and Heather was waiting for the blueberry-swirl cheesecake she'd ordered, Sherry excused herself and retreated to the ladies' room. She applied fresh lipstick and lingered. She was uncertain of so many things. Cody had told her how much he *didn't* want to be attracted to her, and she'd found his words faintly insulting. Now she understood. She was attracted to him, and she didn't like it, either, didn't know how to deal with it. What troubled her most was that she seemed to be weakening toward him. She'd always thought of herself as strong-willed, but now her defenses were crumbling. She feared that, as the evening progressed, it would become increasingly difficult to hide her feelings—and that could prove disastrous.

Sherry had rejected his less-than-flattering proposal. Cody made it sound as if he was too busy rounding up cattle to date her properly. But it was much more than that. He wasn't willing to make an emotional commitment to her and their relationship, and Sherry would accept nothing less.

She was on her way back into the dining room when a tall, vaguely familiar-looking man approached her.

His eye caught hers, and he hesitated a moment before speaking.

"Excuse me," he said, smiling apologetically, "but don't I know you?"

Sherry studied him, sharing the same feelings, but unable to decide where or when she'd met him. "I'm not from this area," she said. "This is my first time in Abilene."

He frowned and introduced himself, but that didn't help. "It'll come to me. Do I look familiar to you?"

Sherry studied him. "A little, but I can't place you."

"Or me you. I'm sorry to have disturbed you."

"No problem."

When she reached the table, Cody's eyes were filled with questions. "Do you know that man?"

"I'm not sure. He said his name was Jack Burnside." She paused. "He thought we'd met before. We might have, but neither of us can remember when or where. I'm generally good about remembering people. It's a little embarrassing."

Cody snickered. "Don't you know a come-on when you hear one? That guy's never met you—he was just looking for an excuse to introduce himself. His ploy's as old as the hills. I thought you were smarter than that."

"Apparently not," Sherry admitted, refusing to allow Cody the pleasure of irritating her.

"I think you should dance with Sherry," Heather suggested once more, glancing at the minuscule dance floor where several other couples were swaying to the music.

"I'm sure your father would rather we—"

"As it happens, I'd be more than happy to give it a try." Cody's gaze seemed to hold a challenge.

Sherry blinked. Cody had managed to surprise her once again. She stood when he pulled out her chair. His hand felt warm at the small of her back as he guided her to the polished wooden floor.

He turned her into his arms with a bit of flair, causing her skirt to fan out from her knees. Then he brought her close to him, so close she was sure she could feel his heart beating.

Sherry wasn't fooled; she knew exactly what he was doing, although she doubted he'd ever admit it. He hadn't asked her to dance because of any great desire to twirl her around the floor, but to make sure Jack Burnside understood she was with him. He was placing his brand on her.

His attitude angered her, yet in some odd way pleased her, too. She was gratified to realize the attraction was mutual.

While Cody may have escorted her onto the dance floor to indicate clearly she was with *him,* Sherry was convinced he was as unprepared as she was for the impact of the physical closeness. His hold on her gradually grew more possessive. His hand slid upward from the dip of her waist until his fingers were splayed across her back. Of its own volition, her head moved closer to his until her temple rested against the lean strength of his jaw. Her eyes drifted closed, and she breathed in the scent of spicy after-shave. The music was pleasant, easy and undemanding. Romantic.

As soon as she realized what she was doing, allowing herself to be drawn into the magic of the moment, she pulled her head away from his and concentrated on the music. Cody didn't attempt anything beyond a mere shuffling of his feet, which suited Sherry just fine.

She quickly saw her mistake. With her head back, their eyes inevitably met, and neither seemed inclined to look away. They continued to gaze at each other, attempting to gauge all that remained unspoken between them. The longer they continued to stare at each other the more awkward it became. Warm seconds ripened into warmer minutes....

It was Sherry who could bear it no longer, who was the first to look away. Cody's hand eased her head back toward his, and she sighed as her temple again unerringly came to rest against his jaw. Her eyes had just drifted shut when, out of the blue, she remembered where she'd met Jack Burnside.

"College," she said abruptly, freeing herself from Cody's embrace. She glanced about the restaurant until she spotted Jack. "I do know him," she said. "We met in Seattle several years ago." Taking Cody by the hand, she led him off the dance floor to a table at the far side of the restaurant, where Jack was eating alone. He stood at their approach.

"Jack," she said, slightly breathless, "you're right, we do know each other. I'm Sherry Waterman. Your sister and I were roommates in our junior year at college. You were in Seattle on business and took us both to dinner. That must have been eight or more years ago now."

Jack's face broke into a wide grin. "Of course. You're Angela's friend. I was certain we'd met."

"Me, too, but I couldn't remember where."

"So, how are you?"

"Fine," Sherry replied, "I'm living in Texas now."

"As a matter of fact, so am I. Small world, isn't it?" His gaze moved fleetingly to Cody.

"Very small," Sherry agreed.

Jack seemed especially pleased to have made the connection. "I never forget a face, especially one as pretty as yours."

Sherry blushed at the compliment. "This is Cody Bailman."

The two men exchanged brisk handshakes. "Please join me," Jack invited, gesturing toward the empty chairs at his table.

"Thanks, but no," said Cody. "My daughter is with us and she's rather shy. She'd be uncomfortable around a stranger, I'm afraid." Cody refused to meet Sherry's baffled glance. Heather—shy?

The three of them spoke briefly for a few minutes longer, and then Sherry and Cody returned to their table and an impatient Heather.

Sherry knew that the reason she'd dragged Cody off the dance floor was more than the opportunity to prove she was right about Jack. It was a means of breaking the romantic spell they'd found themselves under. Cody had made her feel vulnerable, and she'd seized the opportunity to show him she was not.

"Who were you talking to?" Heather asked, craning her neck. "I didn't think you two were ever going to come back."

"The man who approached me earlier," said Sherry. "I remembered who he was, so we went over to speak to him. He's a friend of mine. Actually, his sister and I are friends. Jack and I only met once."

"Apparently your time with him was memorable," said Cody. Sherry caught the hint of sarcasm in his voice and was amused.

He paid the tab, and the three of them began to head out of the dining room. Cody glanced in Jack's direction, then back to Sherry, and said stiffly, "You're welcome to stay and visit with your friend, if you like."

"I've visited enough, thanks," she said, following him and Heather to the elevators.

They weren't back in the suite more than thirty seconds before Heather changed out of her dress and into her pajamas and new fuzzy slippers. The girl plopped herself down in front of the television set, studying the movie guide. She checked out her selection with Cody, who gave his approval.

Sherry changed out of the evening gown and into a comfortable pair of jeans and a cotton T-shirt, then wandered back into the living room to sit on the sofa with Heather. Her mind wasn't on the first-run movie the girl had opted for; it was on Cody and what had transpired between them while they were dancing.

When they'd left Pepper, the emotional distance between them had felt as wide and deep as the Grand Canyon. Now she wasn't sure what to think. She glanced at him. He was sitting at the table, with his briefcase open in front of him. He reached for the phone and ordered a pot of coffee from room service.

What made matters so difficult was how strongly she was attracted to him. It saddened her to realize there was little chance for a truly loving relationship between them. His life was ranching. He needed a woman in his life to appease Heather—though certainly there were beneficial side effects. It wouldn't be a one-sided relationship. Cody would be generous with her in every way except the one that mattered. With himself.

Sherry wanted a man who cherished her, a man who was willing to do whatever was necessary to win her heart, even if it meant courting her during the busiest time of the year. She wanted a husband who would withhold none of himself from her. And Cody couldn't offer that.

"Something troubling you?" he asked, looking up from his paperwork.

The question snapped her out of her reverie. "No," she said abruptly. "What makes you ask?"

"You look like you're about to cry."

Strangely that was exactly how she felt. She managed a chuckle. "Don't be silly."

Heather fell asleep halfway through the movie. When Cody noticed his daughter had curled up on the sofa and nestled her head in Sherry's lap, he stood, and turned off the TV after a nod from Sherry, and gently lifted the twelve-year-old into his arms. Heather stirred and opened her eyes as if she wanted to scold him for treating her like a little girl, but she must have thought better of it for she let him carry her to bed.

Sherry pulled back the covers, and Cody gently placed his daughter, who seemed to have fallen right back to sleep, on the mattress. Silently they moved from the room and then paused as if each was suddenly aware they were now alone.

Luckily Sherry had remembered to bring a book along with her, and she opted to sit on the couch and bury herself in it. Although Cody sat at the table to the side, busy with his own affairs, Sherry had never been more aware of him. Agreeing to the suite had been a mistake. She should have insisted upon two rooms on different floors.

"Would you like some coffee?" Cody's question cut into the silence.

"No, thanks." If it wasn't so early, she'd make her excuses and go to bed too, but it would look ridiculous for her to turn in at nine-thirty.

Unexpectedly Cody released a beleaguered sigh. "All right," he said, "let's air this once and for all and be done with it."

"Air what?" she asked, innocently.

"What's happening between us."

"I wasn't aware anything was now."

He closed his briefcase with a deliberate lack of haste, then stood and walked over to the sofa. He sat down on the end opposite her, as far removed from her as he could get and still be on the same piece of furniture. "I've had more than a week to give your rejection of my proposal ample consideration."

Sherry spoke softly. "I shouldn't have said what I did."

He brightened and cocked his head as if he thought it was about time she'd shown some sense. "You mean you've changed your mind and decided to marry me?"

"No." She didn't like to be so blunt, but it seemed the only way to reach Cody. "I regret saying I'd rather eat fried rattlesnake."

"Oh." His shoulders slumped. "I should have known it wouldn't be that easy," he muttered. He reached for a pen and pad. "All right, I'd like to know exactly what it is you find so objectionable about me."

"Nothing, really. You're honest, hardworking, trustworthy. My grandmother, if she were alive, would call you a salt-of-the-earth kind of guy, and I'd agree with her. It would be very easy to fall in love with you, Cody. Sometimes I think I already have, and that terrifies me."

"Why?" His expression was sincere.

"Because you don't love me."

His face fell. "I *like* you. I'm attracted to you. That's a hell of a lot more than many other couples start out with."

"Love frightens you, doesn't it? You lost Heather's mother, and you've guarded your heart ever since."

"Don't be ridiculous." He stood and walked to the window, stuffing his hands in his pants pockets and staring out at the night. His back was to her, but that didn't prevent Sherry from hearing the pain in his voice. "Karen died ten years ago. I hardly even remember what she looked like anymore." He turned to gaze at her. "That's the problem with you women. You read a few magazine articles and romance novels and then think you're experts on relationships."

"You loved her, didn't you?"

"Of course, and I grieved when she died."

"You opted not to remarry," she told him softly, afraid of agitating him further.

"I didn't have the time, and to be truthful, my life was plenty full without letting a woman dominate my time. That's why I want to set the record straight right now. I'm not about to let a wife put a collar around my neck and lead me around like a puppy."

"Karen did that?"

"No." He scowled fiercely. "But I've seen it happen to plenty of other men, including Luke."

"Ellie doesn't seem the type to do such a thing."

Cody frowned. "I know—Luke put the collar around his own neck." He walked over to the table, made a notation on the pad and glanced her way. "I was thinking you and I might reach some sort of compromise."

"Is that possible?"

"I don't know," he answered. "But it might be if we try."

"Before we go any further, I want it understood I have no intention of changing who you are, Cody. That's not what marriage is about."

His look told her he didn't believe her. Sherry, however, had no intention of arguing with him. He'd believe whatever he wanted.

"Already this isn't working," Cody said, brushing the hair from his face in an agitated movement. "I was hoping to make a list, so I'd know exactly what it is you want from me."

"For what?"

He slapped the pen he still held on top of the table. "So we can be done with this foolishness and get married!"

She hadn't meant to be obtuse, but their conversation had taken so many twists she wasn't clear on exactly what it was they were discussing.

"You still want to marry me?"

"Obviously, otherwise I wouldn't be willing to make a fool of myself a second time."

"Why?" she asked, genuinely curious.

"Damned if I know," he snapped. He took a moment to compose himself and come to grips with his temper. "Because I like the way you feel in my arms. I like the way you taste. Your mouth is sweet, and kissing you reminds me of eating an orange when it's ripe and juicy. It's the kind of kiss a man could get addicted to."

"That's all?" she asked.

"No. I also want to marry you because my daughter clearly adores you. On top of that, you're not hard on the eyes, you're intelligent and well-read."

"Ah," Sherry said.

Her response seemed to succeed in making him angrier. "Dammit, there's electricity between us—you can't deny it."

This man had the most uncanny way of insulting her with compliments. He made it impossible for her to be angry, and luckily she was more amused than offended.

"We've only kissed on two occasions," she reminded him.

"Only two?" He sounded as if that were impossible. "Well, honey, I guess you pack quite a wallop."

Sherry decided to accept that as a compliment, and she smiled softly. He was in front of her suddenly, his hands reaching for hers, drawing her up so that she stood before him. "I can't stop thinking about how good you taste," he whispered. His mouth was mere inches from her own.

A kiss, Sherry realized, would muddle her reasoning processes, but then again, they were already so tangled it shouldn't matter.

He pulled her closer. For one crazy moment all they did was stare at each other. Then Cody spoke. "It's been a hell of a long time since I've kissed a woman the way I want to kiss you." His words were low and heavy with need.

"I'm not afraid," Sherry said simply.

"Maybe not, but I sure as hell am." His arms went around her, folding her into his chest. How right this felt, Sherry thought. How perfectly their bodies fit together, as if they'd been crafted for one another.

His voice was ragged and oddly breathless when he instructed. "You kiss me."

Sherry didn't hesitate, not for an instant. She placed her hands on either side of his head and drew it down toward hers. Their lips met in an uncomplicated kiss. Sweet, gentle, undemanding. Then it changed in intensity. What had seemed so sweet and simple a moment earlier took on a magnitude and power that left her head swimming and her lungs depleted of air.

Cody groaned and his mouth slanted hard over hers. Sherry felt herself opening up to him in ways she never had before. Her mouth opened to him, her arms and, most frightening of all, her heart.

This wasn't the type of kiss that burned itself out, that made the gradual transformation from passionate to a series of sweet pecks. This kiss was a long way from being complete before it grew too hot, too heady for either of them to handle.

Sherry wasn't sure who moved first, but they broke apart and stepped back. Space, she needed space, and from the look of him, so did Cody. Sherry's chest was heaving, her heart pounding, and her emotions threatened to fly out of control.

Cody spoke first. "I think," he said raggedly, "that it's a fair assumption to say we're sexually compatible."

Sherry nodded mutely. This brief experiment with the physical realm of their relationship proved to be more potent than she'd thought possible. She raised her trembling fingers to her lips and investigated them for herself.

Suddenly, standing seemed to require a great amount of energy, so Sherry moved back to the sofa and sat, hoping she looked composed and confident. She felt neither.

Cody waited a moment, then joined her as he had earlier—on the far end of the sofa where there wasn't any possibility of them accidentally touching.

He reached for the same pad and pencil. "Thus far your main objection to our marrying is..." He hesitated, then reviewed his notes and set aside the pad as if all this was beyond him.

"I want to be sure of something," Sherry said when she was reasonably sure her voice would sound even and steady. "Heather's 4-H project."

Cody's gaze shot to hers, and she read the remorse in their dark depths.

"This sudden desire for a wife—does it have anything to do with that?"

His shoulders squared defensively. "Yes and no. To be fair, I hadn't given much thought to marrying again until this past year, and Heather had a lot to do with that decision. She's at the age now when she needs someone's influence other than Janey's. Someone younger. She realized it herself, I think, before I did.

Otherwise she wouldn't have come up with that crazy project idea.''

"I see." Sherry found the truth painful, but was pleased he hadn't lied.

"But that doesn't mean anything. I didn't meet you and immediately decide you'd be a perfect mother for Heather. I looked at you and decided you were perfect wife for *me,* with one exception."

"What's that?"

"You want everything sugar-coated."

"Cody, it's much more than that."

He shook his head. "I'm not the type to decorate something with a bunch of fancy words. Nor do I have the time to persuade you I'm decent enough to be your husband. If you haven't figured that out by now, then flowers and candy ain't going to do it."

"Don't be so sure," she teased.

"That's what you want, is it?" He was frowning so mightily, his lips were white.

"I want a man who's willing to make an emotional commitment to me, and that includes time to come to know one another properly. I'm not willing to settle for anything less. If you're serious about marrying me, Cody Bailman, then you're going to have to prove to me you're sincere. I'm not willing to accept some . . . some offhand proposal."

Cody muttered something under his breath that Sherry couldn't catch, but from the look of him it was just as well she didn't.

"You're looking for romance, aren't you?" he asked.

"That and much more," she told him, her tone intense. "I need to know I'm important to you, that this attraction isn't just a passing thing."

"I asked you to marry me, didn't I?" He sounded thoroughly disgusted. "Trust me, a man doesn't get any more serious than that."

"Perhaps not," Sherry agreed. "But a woman needs a little more than a proposal that talks about cutting to the chase and being done with it."

"You want me down on one knee with my heart on my sleeve, telling you I couldn't survive without you?"

She considered that for a moment. "That would be a good start."

"I thought so." Cody stood and marched over to his briefcase. He cast his pen and pad inside, then slammed down the lid. "Well, you can forget it. I'm willing to compromise, but that's as far as it goes. Take it or leave it, the choice is up to you."

Sherry closed her eyes to her mounting frustration. "I believe we've both made our choices."

CHAPTER SEVEN

SHERRY SAT in a booth at the Yellow Rose, sipping coffee and mulling over the events of the weekend in Abilene. Doubts assailed her from all sides. Twice now, her heart in her throat, she'd rejected Cody's marriage proposal.

The irony of the situation didn't escape her. For years she'd longed for a husband and family. She'd been looking for a change in her life. This was the very reason she'd uprooted herself and moved halfway across the country.

She'd been in Texas less than a month, and in that time she'd been held captive by a community, helped deliver a beautiful baby boy and received a marriage proposal. This was some kind of state.

Cody. She wished she could think clearly about him. That she'd meet a man who attracted her so powerfully came as a shock. That he should feel equally captivated by her was an unexpected bonus.

Donna Jo strolled over to the booth and refilled her coffee. "You're looking a little under the weather," the friendly waitress commented. "How'd your weekend with Cody and Heather go?"

It was no surprise that Donna Jo knew she'd spent the weekend with the Bailmans. "We had a lot of fun."

Donna Jo set the glass pot on the table and pressed her hands into her hips. She shifted her weight from one foot to the other as if what she had to say was of momentous importance. "Take my word, honey, that man's sweet on you."

Sherry's only response was a weak smile. "I heard about Heather's 4-H project. That's what you and Mrs. Colson wanted me to find out on my own, wasn't it?"

Donna Jo did a poor job of hiding her amusement. "I wondered how long it'd take for you to learn about that. Cody's kid's got a good head on her shoulders. Heather figured that suggesting she find him a wife herself guaranteed her father's attention, and by golly she was right." Donna Jo laughed at the memory. "Cody was shocked. He's lived so long without a woman that I don't think remarrying so much as entered his mind. You're sweet on him, too, aren't you?'

"He's a good man." Sherry tried to sound noncommittal.

"Cody's one of the best. He can be cantankerous, but then he wouldn't be a man if he wasn't. Now, I don't have any dog in this fight, but—"

Sherry stopped her. "You don't have a dog? They fight dogs in Texas?"

"Of course not. It's an old Texan saying, meaning I don't have a stake in what happens between you and Cody. I've been married a whole lot of years myself, and personally I'd like to see Cody find himself a decent wife." Her smile widened. "Folks in the Yellow Rose been talking about you two, and everyone agrees Cody should marry you. Are we going to have a fall wedding?"

"Uh..."

"Leave Doc's helper alone," the sheriff called out from his perch at the counter, "and bring that coffee over here."

"Hold your horses, Billy Bob. This is the kind of information folks come into the Yellow Rose for. Trust me, it isn't the liver-and-onion special they're after, it's gossip, and everyone wants to know what's happening between Cody and Sherry."

It seemed everyone in the café was staring at Sherry, expecting a response.

"I hear you and Heather traveled with him to Abilene." The sheriff said, twisting around to face her. "That sounds promising. Right promising."

"Sure does," someone else agreed.

"The way I see it," said a second man—Sherry hadn't formally met him, but she knew he was the local minister "—a man wasn't meant to be alone, a woman neither. Now I know there're plenty of folks who'd argue with me, but it seems if you're both wanting the same thing, then you should get on with it."

With everyone looking at her so expectantly, Sherry felt obligated to say something, anything. "I... Thanks for the advice. I'll take it into consideration." She couldn't get out of the café fast enough. It seemed everyone had a curious question or some tidbit of wisdom.

By the time Sherry reached the clinic, she regretted opening her mouth. She had no idea so many people would be interested in what was happening between her and Cody.

Mrs. Colson looked up from her desk when Sherry came through the front door. "Good morning," the receptionist greeted cheerfully, her gaze full of questions.

"Morning," Sherry said, hurrying past. Her eagerness to escape didn't go unnoticed.

"How was your weekend with Cody and Heather?" Mrs. Colson craned her neck and called after her.

"Great." Sherry reached behind the examination room door for her jacket and was buttoning up the front when the receptionist let herself in. "I heard first thing this morning that Cody popped the question. I don't even think Donna Jo's heard this yet. Is it true?"

Sherry's hands fumbled with the last button and her heart zoomed straight to her knees. "Who told you that?"

"Oh, you know—the grapevine."

"You should know by now how unreliable that can be," Sherry said as unemotionally as she could, unwilling to swallow the bait.

Mrs. Colson wiggled her brows. "Not this time. My source is pure as the driven snow. I have my ways of learning certain things."

"This town's worse than Orchard Valley," Sherry muttered. "I barely know Cody Bailman. What makes you think he'd ask a casual acquaintance to marry him, and furthermore, what makes you assume I'd accept?"

"Casual acquaintance, is it?" Mrs. Colson asked, tapping her index finger against her lips. "It seems to me you know him well enough to dance cheek to cheek in some fancy hotel restaurant, don't you?"

"You know about that, too?" Sherry's lower jaw dropped. "Is nothing sacred in this town?"

"Morning." Doc Lindsey strolled into the room, and spying Sherry, he paused and grinned broadly. "I hear you're marrying Cody Bailman. He's a damn good man. He'll make you a good husband." He patted Sherry's back and sauntered out of the room.

Sherry balled her hands into fists and looked toward the ceiling while she counted to ten. Apparently the folks in Pepper had nothing better to do than speculate on Cody's love life.

"Cody's waited a long time to find the right woman," Mrs. Colson stated matter-of-factly on her way out the door. "I only hope his stubbornness doesn't ruin everything."

"Mrs. Colson," Sherry said, placing the stethoscope around her neck. "I don't mean to be rude or unfriendly, but I'd rather not discuss my personal affairs with you or Donna Jo, or Billy Bob or anyone else."

"The mayor's got a good ear if you change your mind."

Sherry grit her teeth in her effort not to lose her temper. Something was going to have to be said, and soon; the situation was getting totally out of hand.

Sherry saw several patients that morning, the majority for physicals before the start of the school year, which was only a week away. Rather than risk another confrontation with Donna Jo and the lunch crowd at the Yellow Rose, she ordered a chef salad and had it delivered.

At one, Mrs. Colson ushered her into Doc's office, where a tall, regal-looking older woman in a lovely blue suit was waiting for her. The woman's hair was white with a smattering of gray, and she wore it in an elegant French roll.

"Hello," Sherry said. The woman sat, her legs crossed at the ankle, her designer purse clenched in her lap.

"You must be Sherry. I'm Judith Bailman, Cody's mother. I've made the trip from Dallas to meet you."

Sherry felt an overwhelming urge to sit down. "I'm pleased to make your acquaintance, Mrs. Bailman."

"The pleasure is mine. I understand there are several items we need to discuss."

For the life of her, Sherry couldn't make her mouth work. She twisted around and pointed toward the door in a futile effort to explain that she was on duty. Unfortunately, no patients were waiting at the moment.

"Mrs. Colson's arranged for us to have several minutes of privacy, so you needn't worry we'll be interrupted."

"I see." Sherry claimed Doc's chair, on the other side of the desk, nearly falling into it. "What can I do for you, Mrs. Bailman?"

"I understand my son's proposed to you?" She eyed Sherry speculatively.

Sherry didn't mean to sound curt, but after everything else that had happened that day, she was in no mood to review her private life with anyone. "I believe that's between Cody and me."

"I quite agree. I don't mean to be nosy. I hope you'll forgive me. It's just that Cody's been single all these years, so I couldn't help getting excited when Heather mentioned—"

"Heather?" Sherry interrupted. That explained everything.

"Why, yes. My granddaughter phoned me first thing this morning." A smile tempted the edges of her mouth. "She's concerned her father's going to ruin her best chance at being a big sister, and knowing my son, I strongly suspect she's right."

"Mrs. Bailman—"

"Please, call me Judith."

"Judith," Sherry said, "don't get me wrong, I think the world of Cody and Heather. Your son did ask me to marry him in a sort of offhand cavalier way."

The woman's mouth tightened. "That sounds like Cody."

"If you must know, I turned him down. Cody makes marriage sound about as appealing as a flu shot."

Judith laughed softly. "I can see I'm going to like you, Sherry Waterman."

"Thank you." She wasn't accustomed to having an entire town and now the man's mother involved in her affairs. At least when she lived in Orchard Valley, her life was mostly her own. It seemed that the minute she'd been hired to work in Pepper, her personal business was up for grabs.

"I hope you'll forgive me for being so blunt, but are you in love with Cody?"

Sherry meant to explain that she was strongly attracted to Judith's son, then add how much she respected and liked him, but instead, she found herself nodding.

The full impact of the truth took her by storm. She closed her eyes and waited several moments for the strong waves of emotion to pass.

Judith smiled and sighed with apparent relief. "I guessed as much. I tried speaking to him about you, but he refused. If the truth be known, I would have been surprised had he listened," she muttered. "That boy's more stubborn than a mule and always has been."

The description was apt, and Sherry found herself smiling.

"If he knew I was here, I don't know he'd ever forgive me, so I'm going to have to ask for your discretion."

"Of course." Sherry glanced worriedly at the door.

"You needn't worry that Martha Colson will say anything. We've been friends for years." She sighed and looked past Sherry and out the window. "Be patient with him, Sherry. He's closed himself off from love, and knowing him the way I do, he's fighting his feelings for you with the full strength of his will. Which, I might add, is formidable."

How well Sherry knew. She'd bumped heads with it more than once, and each time she'd come away shaken.

"Cody deserves your love," Judith said softly. "Sure he has his faults, but believe me, the woman my son loves will be happy. When he falls in love again, it'll be with his whole heart and soul. It may take some time, but I promise you the wait will be well worth the effort."

Sherry wasn't sure how to respond. "I'll remember that."

"Now—" Judith gave a deep sigh and stood "—I must be on my way. Remember, not a word of my visit to either my son or granddaughter."

"I promise."

Judith hugged her and said softly. "Be patient with Cody. He'll make you a wonderful husband."

"I'll try," Sherry promised.

Cody's mother left by the back door. When Mrs. Colson returned, her sparkling eyes met Sherry's and she said, "This visit will be our little secret."

"What visit?" she answered.

FRIDAY EVENING, Sherry sat out on the porch in front of the clinic enjoying the coolness. The wooden bench swung gently in the breeze, creaking now and again. Crickets telegraphed greetings to one another, the sound almost musical in the still of the night.

Evenings were her favorite time. Sherry loved to sit outside and think about her day. Her life was falling into a pattern now as she adjusted to the good people of Pepper. Often she read, or wrote letters home, mentioning as Norah had done the peculiarities she saw in day-to-day life in the Lone Star state. No doubt she was the peculiar one with her Northern ways, but folks here had accepted her readily. Norah's birthday was coming up soon, and Sherry had spent the earlier part of the evening writing her a long, chatty letter.

Her heart seemed to skip a beat when Cody's pickup eased to a stop in front of the clinic. She stood and walked over to the steps, leaning against the support beam while he climbed out of the cab and came toward her.

"Hi, Sherry," he said, looking a bit sheepish. He stopped in front of the gate.

"Hi, Cody."

He stared at her for several seconds as if trying to remember the purpose of his visit. Sherry decided to make it easier for him. "Would you care to sit a spell?" She motioned toward the swing.

"Don't mind if I do." He'd recently shaved and the familiar scent of his after-shave floated past her as he moved to the swing.

They sat side by side, swaying gently back and forth. Neither seemed eager to talk.

"I was on my way to playing poker with a few friends," he said at last, "when I saw you sitting here."

"I do most evenings. Nights are so beautiful. I love stargazing. It's one of the reasons I'd never be happy in a big city. Sometimes the sky's so full it's impossible to look away."

"Have you had a good week?" he asked.

"A busy one. What about you?"

"The same." His gaze found hers. "Any problems?"

"Such as?"

He shrugged and looked past her to the street. "I thought there might have been some talk about, you know, us."

"There was definitely some heavy speculation after our trip last weekend."

"Anyone pestering you?"

"Not really. What about you?"

He laughed lightly. "You mean other than Heather and Janey?"

The bench squeaked in the quiet that followed.

"I've been thinking about what you said about romance," he admitted after a moment.

"Oh?"

"To my way of thinking, it's pure foolishness."

Sherry frowned. "So you've said." Countless times, but reminding him of that would have sounded petty and argumentative. The moment was peaceful, and she didn't want to ruin it.

"Tell me what you want and I'll do it." He said decisively, as if he was filling an order for ranching supplies.

"You want a list?"

"It'd help. I'm not much good at this sort of thing, and I'm going to need a few instructions."

Sherry turned to look at him. She pressed her hand to his cheek and held it there. "That's really very sweet, Cody. I'm touched."

"If that's the only way I can convince you to marry me, then what the hell, I'll do it. Just tell me what it is you want, so I don't waste a lot of time."

Sherry wasn't sure what to say. "I . . . I hate to disappoint you, but having me give you instructions would ruin it. It has to come from your heart, Cody." She moved her hand to his chest and pressed it there. "Otherwise it wouldn't be sincere."

A frown quickly snapped into place. "You want me to do a few mushy things to prove my feelings are sincere, but you aren't willing to tell me what they are?"

"You make it sound silly."

"As far as I'm concerned, it is. Damnation, woman, you seem to think I'm a mind reader. Well, I've had about all the—"

Their peace was about to be destroyed, and Sherry was unwilling to let it happen. So she acted impulsively and stopped him the only way she knew would work.

She kissed him.

The instant her mouth covered his, she felt his anger melt away. His arms gripped her shoulders and his kiss was both tender and fierce. His breath was warm and his lips hot and eager, and the kiss left her trembling.

Then he began kissing her neck, from the underside of her chin to the top of her slender shoulder. As always happened when he touched her, Sherry felt like Dorothy caught up in the tornado, her world spinning out of control, before landing in a magical land. When he raised his head from hers, she was left feeling utterly bereft.

Cody started to say something, then changed his mind. He raised his finger to her face and brushed it down her cheek. "I have to go."

She wanted him to stay, but wouldn't ask it of him.

"The fellows are waiting for me. They're counting on me."

"It's all right, Cody. I understand."

He stood and stuffed his hands in his jeans pockets, as if to stop himself from reaching for her a second time. The thought that this was probably the case helped lighten the melancholy she experienced at his leaving.

"It was good to see you again," he said stiffly.

"Good to see you, too," she returned just as stiffly.

He hesitated at the top step and turned back to face her. "Uh, you're sure you don't want to give me a few tips on, you know, romance?"

"I'm confident you aren't going to need them. Follow your heart, Cody, and I promise you it'll lead directly to mine."

He smiled, and Sherry swore she'd never seen anything sexier.

SHE DIDN'T HEAR from Cody all day Saturday, which was disappointing. She'd hoped he'd taken her words to heart and understood what she'd been trying to say.

Yes, she wanted to be wooed, courted the way women had been courted for centuries. But she also wanted to be loved. Cody was more afraid of love than he was marriage.

Late that night when she was in bed reading, she heard something or someone outside her bedroom window. At first she didn't know what to make of it. The noise was awful, loud and discordant as if someone was rocking a chair over a cat's tail. Several moments passed before she realized it was someone playing a guitar, or rather, attempting to play a guitar.

She reached over and pulled open the blinds. She stared out to see Cody standing on the lawn in front of her window, crooning for all he was worth.

"Cody," she shouted, jerking up the window and sticking out her head, "what in heaven's name are you doing?"

He started to sing even louder than before. Sherry winced. She couldn't help it. His singing was even worse than his guitar playing. Holding up the window with one hand, she covered her ear with the other.

"Cody," she shouted once more in an attempt to get him to stop.

"You wanted romance," he called back and then repeatedly strummed the guitar in a burst of energy. "Sweetheart, this comes straight from the heart, just the way you wanted."

"Have you been drinking?"

He laughed and tossed back his head, running his fingers over the guitar strings with hurried, unpracticed fingers. "You don't honestly believe I'd attempt this sober, do you?"

"Cody!"

The sound of a police siren in the background startled Sherry. It was the first time she could remember hearing it in Pepper. Apparently there was some kind of trouble, but Sherry didn't have the time to think about that now, not with Cody serenading her, sounding like a sick bull.

"Cody!" she shouted once more.

"What's the matter?" he called back. "You said you wanted romance. Well this is as good as it gets."

"Give me a minute to get dressed and I'll be right out." She started to lower the window, then thought better of it. Sticking her head out again, she brushed the hair away from her face and slowly shook her head. "Don't go away, and for the love of heaven, stop playing that guitar."

"Anything you want," he said strumming for all his worth.

Even lowering the window didn't help. Cody knew as much about guitar playing as she did about mustering cattle. Donning jeans and a light sweater, she stuffed her feet into tennis shoes and hurried out the door without bothering to brush her hair.

As she came out onto the front porch, she was gratified to realize he'd stopped playing. It wasn't until she'd reached the bottom step that she noticed the police car was parked in front of the clinic.

Hurrying around to the side of the building, she met up with Cody and a sheriff's deputy. His flashlight was zeroed in on her romantic idiot.

"Is there a problem here?" Sherry asked. She hadn't met this particular deputy, but the small gold name tag above his shirt pocket read Steven Bean.

"No problem, isn't that right, Mr. Bailman?"

"None whatsoever," Cody said, looking as sober as a judge. If it wasn't for the cocky smile he wore, it would have been impossible to know he'd been drinking. "I only had a couple of shots of whiskey," he explained. "It was necessary, or else I'd never have had the guts to pull this off."

"Are you arresting Mr. Bailman?" Sherry asked.

"We had three calls within the last five minutes," Deputy Bean explained. "The first call claimed there was a wounded animal in town. The second one came from Mayor Bowie. He said we had the authority to do whatever was necessary to put an end to that infernal racket. Those were his precise words."

"I may not be another Willie Nelson, but my singing isn't that bad," Cody protested.

"Trust me, Bailman, it's bad. Real bad."

Cody looked to Sherry for vindication. Even though he was serenading her in the name of romance, even though he was suffering this supreme embarrassment on her behalf, she couldn't bring herself to lie.

"I think it'd be better if you didn't sing again for a while," she suggested tactfully.

He gave her an injured look. "Are you going to take me to the jail?" Cody demanded.

"I could, you know," Deputy Bean told him.

"On what grounds?" Sherry challenged.

"Disturbing the peace, for starters."

"I didn't know it was unlawful to play the guitar."

"It is the way you do it," Deputy Bean muttered.

"He won't be doing it again," Sherry promised, looking to Cody for confirmation. "Right?"

"Right." Cody held up his right hand.

The Deputy sighed and lowered his flashlight. "In that case, why don't we drop the whole matter and let it go with a warning."

"Thank you," Sherry said.

The deputy started to turn away, but Cody stopped him. "Will there be a report of this in the paper on Wednesday?"

The officer shrugged. "I suppose. The *Weekly* reports all police calls."

"I'd appreciate it if you could see that this one doesn't make it to the paper."

"I can't do that, Mr. Bailman."

"Why not?"

"I'm not the one who turns the calls over to Mr. Douglas. He comes in every morning and collects them himself."

"Then make sure he doesn't have anything to collect," Cody said.

The deputy shrugged. "I'll do my best, but I'm not making any promises. After all, we got three calls, you know."

Cody waited until the patrol car had disappeared into the night before he removed his Stetson and slammed it against his leg. He stared at his mangled hat and attempted to bend it back into shape.

"I've damn near ruined the best hat I've ever had because of you," he grumbled.

"Me?"

"You heard me."

"Are you blaming me for this . . . this fiasco?"

"No!" he shouted back. "I'm blaming Luke. He was the one who suggested I serenade you. He claimed it didn't matter that I couldn't play the guitar or sing. He said women go crazy for this kind of thing. I should've known." He indignantly brushed off the Stetson before setting it back on his head, adjusting the angle.

"It was very sweet, Cody, and I do appreciate it."

"Sure you do. Women get a real kick out of seeing a grown man make a jackass out of himself in front of the whole town."

"That's not fair!" Sherry protested.

"I'll have you know," Cody barked, waving his arms, "I was well respected and liked in this town before you came along making unreasonable demands on me. All I want is a wife."

"*You're* being unreasonable."

Cody ignored her. "The way I see it, you're waiting for some prince to come along and sweep you away on his big white charger. Well, sweetheart, it isn't going to be me."

For a moment, Sherry was too stunned to respond. "I didn't ask you to serenade me."

"Oh, no," he said, walking away from her. He stopped in front of the gate. "That would have been too easy. On top of everything else, I'm supposed to be psychic. You won't tell me what it is you want. It's up to me to read your mind."

"That's not fair."

"You said it, not me."

"Cody—" She stopped herself, not wanting to argue with him. "Maybe it'd be best if we dropped the whole thing. You're right. I'm way out of line expecting a man who asks me to marry him to love me, too."

Cody apparently didn't hear her, or if he had, he chose to ignore her and the sarcasm. "Luke. That's where I made my mistake," he muttered. "I assumed my best friend would know all the answers, because for all his bumbling ways, he managed to woo Ellie."

"You're absolutely right," Sherry said, marching up the front steps. "You could learn a lesson or two from your friend. At least he was in love with the woman he wanted to marry and wasn't just looking for someone to warm his bed and keep his daughter content."

Cody whirled around and shook his finger at her. "You know what I think?"

"I don't know and I don't really care."

"I'm going to tell you, anyway, so listen."

She crossed her arms and heaved an exasperated sigh.

"Cancel the whole thing!" Cody shouted. "Forget I was fool enough to even ask you to marry me!"

"Cody," someone hollered in the distance. Sherry looked up in time to see a head protruding from the upstairs window of the house across the street. "Either you shut up or I'm calling the sheriff again."

"Don't worry," Cody hollered back, "I'm leaving."

CHAPTER EIGHT

"IS IT TRUE?" Heather asked the following morning as Sherry walked out of church. "Did you nearly get my dad arrested?"

Sherry closed her eyes wearily. "Did Cody tell you that?"

"No." Heather's eyes were huge and round. "I heard Mrs. Ellis telling Mrs. James about it. They said Dad was standing under your bedroom window singing and playing the guitar. I didn't even know Dad could play the guitar."

"He can't. I think you should ask your father about what happened last night," Sherry suggested, unwilling to comment further. She couldn't. Cody would find some way of blaming her.

"He didn't come to church this morning. He had Slim drive me into town because he said his head hurt."

Served him right, thought Sherry.

"School starts tomorrow," Heather announced. "Do you want to know what I'm going to wear for the first day? My acid-washed jeans, that lavender T-shirt and my new shoes."

"Sounds perfect," Sherry told her.

"I've got to go." Heather glanced across the parking lot. "Slim's in the pickup waiting. When are you going to come out to the house again? I was kind of hoping you would last week. I was thinking of having my hair cut and found this rad style in my friend Carrie's magazine. I wanted to show it to you."

"Ask your father if you can stay after school one afternoon this week, and I'll drive you home," Sherry suggested. "But tell him—" she hesitated, "—I won't be able to stay. Be sure he knows that. I'll drop you off and be gone."

"Okay," Heather said, walking backward for several steps. "That'd be really great. Do you mind if my friend Carrie comes along? She wants to meet you, too, and her ranch isn't all that far from mine."

"Sure."

"Thanks." Heather's smile rivaled the afternoon sun. "I'll call and let you know which day."

Sherry waved and the girl raced toward the pickup. Sighing, Sherry started toward her own car. She hadn't gone more than a few steps when she heard Ellie Johnson call her.

"Sherry," Ellie said, walking toward her. "It's good to see you."

"You too."

"I've been meaning to call on you all week, but with the baby and everything else, it slipped my mind. I know it's short notice, but I'd love for you to come over to the house for dinner tonight—I've got a roast in the slow cooker. Luke's so busy these days I'm starved for companionship."

"I'd love to."

"That's great." Ellie seemed genuinely pleased. "You won't have any problems finding your way, will you?"

Sherry was sure she wouldn't. As it happened she was eager for a bit of female companionship. With Ellie, Sherry could be herself. She didn't worry that she'd have to suffer an inquisition or make explanations for herself and Cody.

When Sherry arrived at the ranch an hour or so later, Ellie came out onto the porch to greet her. Year-old Christina Lynn was thrilled to have company, and she raced excitedly.

After giving Ellie's daughter the proper attention, Sherry asked about Philip. "He's sleeping," she was assured. "I fed him and put him down. Christina Lynn's due for her nap, too, but I promised her she could visit with you first." The friendly toddler climbed into Sherry's lap and investigated, with small probing fingers, the jeweled pin she wore.

It had been several weeks now since Sherry had spent time with Norah and her little ones, and she'd forgotten how much she enjoyed children. Christina Lynn seemed equally infatuated with her.

While Sherry devoted herself to the world of a small child, Ellie poured them tall glasses of iced tea and delivered them to the kitchen table.

"I suppose you heard what happened?" Sherry asked, needing to discuss the events of the night before. After all, there was sure to be some sort of backlash, since Cody seemed to blame Luke as much as he did her.

"There were rumors at church this morning. Is it true Cody was nearly arrested?"

"Yes. For disturbing the peace."

A smile wobbled at the edges of Ellie's mouth. "Serves him right. I'm afraid Cody Bailman has several lessons yet to learn when it comes to wooing a woman.''

"I would have thought his first wife, Karen, had taught him all this."

"I never knew her, of course," Ellie said, reaching for her sweating glass, "but apparently Luke did. I asked him about her once."

"What did he tell you?" Sherry was more than curious. The key to understanding Cody was rooted in his first marriage, however brief.

"From what I remember, Cody met Karen while in college. He was away from home for the first time and lonely. Luke was surprised when he married her—at least that's what he told me. She was something of a tomboy, even at twenty. In many ways I suspect she was the perfect rancher's wife. She loved riding the range and working with the cattle. The way I hear it there wasn't anything she couldn't do." Ellie hesitated and looked away as if carefully judging her words. "Luke also said Karen wasn't much of a wife or mother. She resented having to stay home with the baby.

"From what Luke told me they had some drag-out fights about it. Karen died in a car accident after one of them. She threatened to leave Cody and Heather, but Luke doubts she was sincere. She mentioned divorce on a regular basis, dramatically packing her bags and lugging them out to the car. No one will ever know if she meant it that time or not because she took a curve too fast and ran off the road. She died instantly."

"How sad."

"I know Cody loved Karen," Ellie continued. "I admire him for picking up the pieces of his life and moving forward."

"I do, too. I didn't realize his first marriage had been so traumatic."

"It wasn't always unhappy. Don't misunderstand me. Cody cared deeply for his wife, but I don't think he was ever truly comfortable with her, if you know what I mean."

Sherry wasn't sure that she did, but she let it pass.

"He's at a loss when it comes to showing a woman how he feels now. The only woman he ever loved was so involved in herself that there was little love left over for anyone else, including him or Heather."

"He's afraid," Sherry whispered, and for none of the reasons she'd assumed. After learning he was a widower, Sherry believed he'd buried himself in his grief. Now she understood differently. Cody feared if he loved again, that love would come back to him empty and shallow.

"Be patient with him," Ellie advised.

Sherry smiled. "It's funny you should say that. A few days ago someone else said the same thing."

"Cody's so much like Luke. I'd like to shake the pair of them. Luke was the same way when we first met. He assumed that if he loved me he'd lose a part of himself. He put on this rough-and-tough exterior and was so unbelievably unreasonable that . . . suffice to say we had our ups and downs, as well."

"What was the turning point for you and Luke?"

Ellie leaned back in her chair, her expression thoughtful. "My first inclination is to say everything changed when I decided to leave Pepper. That's when

Luke raced after my car on his horse and proposed, but it happened about a week before then." She sighed and sipped her tea. "To hear Luke tell it, we fell in love the moment we set eyes on each other. Trust me, it didn't happen like that. For most of the summer we did little more than argue. He seemed to think I was his exclusive property, which infuriated me."

"What happened?"

"Oh, there wasn't any big climactic scene when we both realized we were destined for each other. In fact, it was something small that convinced me of his love—and eventually mine for him.

"Luke had taken me horseback riding, and I'd dared him to do something stupid. I can't even remember what it was now, but he refused, rightly so, I should add, but it made me mad, so I took off in a gallop. I'm not much of a horsewoman and hadn't gone more than a few feet before I was thrown. Luckily I wasn't hurt, but my pride had taken a beating and Luke made the tragic mistake of laughing at me.

"I was so furious I took off, deciding I'd rather walk back to the ranch than ride. Naturally, it started to rain—heavily—and I was drenched in seconds, Luke, too. I was so angry with him and myself I refused to speak to him. Finally Luke got down off his horse and walked behind me, leading the two mares. He wouldn't leave me, although heaven knew I deserved it. I thought about that incident for a long time afterward, and I realized this was the kind of man I wanted to spend the rest of my life with."

"But you decided to leave Pepper shortly after that."

"Yes," Ellie admitted cheerfully. "It was the only way. He seemed to think marriage was something we could discuss in three or four years."

"It's something Cody wants to discuss every three or four minutes."

Ellie laughed. "Do you love him?"

"Yes," Sherry agreed softly. "But that's not the problem."

"Cody's the problem. I know what you mean."

"He wants me to marry him, but he doesn't want to get emotionally involved with me. He makes the whole thing sound like a business proposition, and I'm looking for much more than a . . . an arrangement."

"You frighten him."

"Good, because he frightens me, too. We met that first day I arrived in town, and my life hasn't been the same since."

Ellie patted Sherry's hand. "Tell me, what's all this business about your insisting upon romance? I overheard Cody talking to Luke yesterday afternoon. I wish I could've recorded the conversation, because it was really very funny. Luke was advising Cody on a variety of ways to win your heart."

"That's the problem. Cody already has my heart. He just doesn't know what to do with it."

"Give him time," Ellie suggested. "Cody's smarter than he looks."

A little later, Sherry helped her friend with the dinner preparations. Christina Lynn awoke from her nap and gleefully "helped" Sherry arrange the silverware around the table. A few minutes before four, Luke returned home, looking hot and dusty. He kissed his wife and daughter, showered and joined them for dinner.

They sat around the big kitchen table and after the blessing, Luke, handing Sherry the bowl of mashed potatoes, said, "I understand Cody came to see you last night." He cast a triumphant smile at his wife. His cocky grin suggested that if Sherry and Cody wed anytime soon, he'd readily accept the credit for getting them together.

"Honey," Ellie said brightly, "Luke was nearly arrested for disturbing the peace. From what Sherry told me, Cody blames you."

"Me? I wasn't the one out there making a first-class fool of myself."

"True, but you were the one who suggested he do it."

"That shouldn't make any difference." Luke ladled gravy over his meat and potatoes before reaching for the green beans. "As long as Sherry was impressed with his romantic soul, it shouldn't matter." He glanced at Sherry and nodded as if to accept her gratitude.

"Well, yes, it was, uh . . ."

"Romantic," Luke supplied, looking hopeful.

"It was romantic, yes."

"It was ridiculous," Ellie inserted.

"A man's willing to do ridiculous things for a woman if that's what she wants."

"I don't, and I never said I did," Sherry was quick to inform the rancher. "It bothers me that Cody would think I wanted him to do anything so . . ."

"Asinine," Ellie supplied.

"Exactly."

Luke was grinning from ear to ear. "Isn't love grand?"

"No, it isn't," a male voice boomed from the doorway. It was Cody, standing on the other side of the screen. He swung it open and stepped inside, eyeing Luke as if he was a traitor who ought to be dragged before a firing squad.

"Cody!" Ellie greeted him warmly. "Please join us for dinner?"

"No, thanks, I just ate. I came over to have a little heart-to-heart with Luke. I didn't realize you had company."

"If it makes you uncomfortable, I'll leave," Sherry offered.

"Don't be silly," Ellie whispered.

Cody's gaze swung to Sherry and it seemed to bore into her very soul. He was angry; she could feel it.

"Come in and have a coffee at least," Ellie said, reaching for the pot and pouring him a cup. Cody moved farther into the kitchen and sat down at the table grudgingly.

"I suppose you heard what happened?" Cody's question was directed at Luke and filled with censure. "The next time I need advice about romance, you're the last person I'm gonna see."

Sherry did her best to concentrate on her meal and ignore both men.

"I assumed because you and Ellie were so blissfully in love," Cody went on, "you'd know the secret of keeping a woman happy."

"He does!"

Three pairs of eyes moved to Ellie. "He loves me."

"Love." Cody spat the word as if he found the very sound of it distasteful.

"That could be the reason a smart woman like Sherry hesitates to marry you," Ellie offered.

"I don't suppose she mentioned the fact I've withdrawn my offer. I've decided the whole idea of marriage is a mistake. I don't need a woman to make a fool out of me."

"Not when you do such a good job of it yourself," Ellie said dryly.

Sherry's grip on her fork tightened at the flash of pain that went through her. It hurt her to think she'd come this close to love only to lose it.

"Anyway," Ellie went on, "I'm sorry to hear you've changed your mind, Cody." Then she grinned. "I've got apple pan dowdy for dessert. Would you care for some?"

"Apple pan dowdy?" Cody's eyes lit up. "I imagine I might find room for a small serving."

Sherry wasn't sure how Ellie arranged it, but within a matter of minutes she was alone in the kitchen with Cody. Philip began to cry and Ellie excused herself. Then Luke made some excuse to leave, taking Christina Lynn with him.

"Would you like some more coffee?" Sherry asked.

"Please."

She refilled his cup, then carried the pot back to the warmer. Never had she been more conscious of Cody than at that moment.

"Heather said something about her stopping off and visiting you one day after school." He was holding his mug with both hands and refusing to look at her.

"If you don't object."

"Hell, no. You've been the best thing to happen to that girl in a long time. I never thought it was possible to convince her to wear a dress."

"She just needed a little guidance is all." Sherry moved about the kitchen, clearing off the table and stacking dirty dishes in the sink. At last she said, "I hope that whatever happens between you and me won't affect my relationship with Heather."

"Don't see why it should. I hope you'll always be friends."

"I hope so, too."

They didn't seem to have much to say after that.

Sherry was the first one to venture into conversation again. "I'm sorry about what happened last night."

He shrugged. "I'll get over it some day." The beginnings of a smile touched his mouth. He stood then and carried his mug to the sink. "I need to get back to the ranch. Give Ellie and Luke my regards, will you?"

Sherry nodded, not wanting him to leave but unable to ask him to stay. She walked him to the door. Cody hesitated on the top step and frowned.

"It'd help matters a whole lot if you weren't so damn pretty," he muttered before turning toward his truck. His strides quickly ate up the distance.

"Cody," Sherry called after him, moving out the door and onto the top step. When he turned back to her, she wrapped her arms around her middle and said, "Now *that* was romantic."

"It was? That's the kind of thing you want me to say?"

"Yes," she said.

"But that was simple."

She smiled. "It came from the heart."

He seemed to stiffen. "The heart," he repeated, placing his hand on his chest. He opened the door of his truck, then looked back at her. "Do you want me to say things like 'God robbed heaven of one of its prettiest angels the day you were born' and mushy stuff like that?"

"That's very sweet, Cody, but it sounds like a line that's been used before."

"It has been," he admitted, his eyes warming with silent laughter. "But I figured it couldn't hurt, especially since it's true."

"Now that was nice."

With an easy grace he climbed into the pickup and closed the door. Propping his elbow against the open window, he looked back to her once more, grinning. "Plan on staying for dinner the night you bring Heather home with you."

"All right, I will. Thanks for the invitation."

Sherry watched him drive away. The dust had settled long before she realized she wasn't alone.

"He's coming around," Ellie commented. "I don't think he realizes it himself yet, but he's falling in love with you hook, line and sinker."

It was exactly what Sherry wanted to hear. Hope blossomed within her and she sighed in contentment.

MONDAY EVENING, Sherry was again sitting in the porch swing, at the clinic, contemplating the events of the weekend. She'd written a long letter to her parents, telling them all about Cody and their rocky relationship.

When she saw his Cadillac turn the corner and pull to a stop in front of the clinic, she wasn't sure what to think. Heather leapt out of the passenger's side and raced up the walkway.

"Dad needs you!"

The girl's voice was high and excited, but her smile discounted any real emergency.

"It's nothing, dammit," Cody said, walking toward her. A box of chocolates was clenched under his arm and he held a bouquet of wildflowers, a mixture of bluebonnets and white-and-yellow daisies.

"The flowers are for you," Heather explained. "Dad picked them himself."

"If you don't mind, I prefer to do my own talking," Cody growled. He jerked up the sleeve of his shirt and started scratching at his forearm.

"Both his arms are a real mess," Heather whispered.

"Heather!" Cody barked.

"He's in one of his moods, too."

"Here," Cody said, thrusting the flowers and candy at Sherry.

Sherry was too flabbergasted to respond right away. "Thank you."

"That's real romantic, isn't it?" his daughter prompted. "Dad asked me what I thought was romantic, and I said flowers and chocolate-covered cherries. They're my favorite, and I bet you like them, too."

"I do." She returned her gaze to Cody.

"What did you get into? Why are you so itchy?"

"This is why he needs you," Heather said in a loud whisper. A cutting look from Cody silenced her.

"I picked the flowers myself. The bluebonnets are the state flower, and I thought you might like the daises. They're plentiful enough around here."

"It looks like you might have tangled with something else," she said, reaching for his arm and moving him toward the light so she could get a better view. "Oh, Cody," she whispered when she saw the redness and the swelling.

"Poison ivy," he told her.

"Let me give you something for that."

"He was hoping you would." Heather said. "He's real miserable. But we can't stay long, because I need to get over to Angela Butterfield's house and pick up my algebra book by eight o'clock."

Sherry led Cody into the clinic and brought out a bottle of calamine lotion, swabbing the worst of the swelling with that. She gave him something for the itch, as well.

Heather sat in the corner of the room, the chocolates in her lap. "Janey says you should give Dad an *A* for effort. I think so, too." This last bit was added between bites of candy. "Did you know you can hold the chocolate in your mouth like this—" she demonstrated "—then suck the cherry out and leave the chocolate intact?"

"Heather, I didn't buy those damn chocolate-covered cherries for you," Cody said irritably.

"I know, but Sherry doesn't mind sharing them, do you?"

"Help yourself."

"She already has," Cody muttered.

Sherry put the lotion away while Cody rolled down his sleeves and snapped them closed at the wrists.

"Heather, don't you have something to occupy yourself with outside?"

"No."

"Yes, you do," he said pointedly.

"I do? Oh, I get it, you want some time alone with Sherry. Gee, Dad, why didn't you just say so?"

"I want some time alone with Sherry."

"Great." Heather read her watch. "Is fifteen minutes enough, or do you need longer? Just remember I need to be at Angela's by eight."

Cody sighed expressively, and Sherry could tell his patience was tattered. "Fifteen minutes will be fine. I'll meet you on the porch."

"I can take the chocolates?"

"Heather!"

"All right, all right, I get the message." She tossed him an injured look on her way outside. "I know when I'm not wanted."

"Not soon enough, you don't," her father tossed out after her.

Now that they were alone, Cody didn't seem to know what it was he wanted to say. He paced the room restlessly, without speaking.

"Cody?"

"I'm thinking."

"This sounds serious," Sherry said softly, amused.

"It *is* serious. Sit down." He pulled out a chair, escorted her to it and sat her down, then stood facing her.

"I'm sorry about the poison ivy," Sherry ventured.

He shrugged. "It's my own fault. I should have noticed it, but my head was in the clouds thinking about you."

"I know it's painful."

"It won't be as bad as the razzing I'm going to take when folks learn about this—on top of my behavior last Saturday night."

"Oh, Cody," she whispered, feeling genuinely contrite, knowing her demands that he be romantic had prompted his actions. He was trying hard to give her what she wanted, yet he didn't seem to understand what she was really asking for. Yes, she wanted the sweet endearing things a man did for a woman he was courting, but she wanted him to trust her and open up to her.

"Listen, I know I said I was withdrawing my proposal of marriage, but we both know I wasn't serious."

Sherry hadn't known that at all, but was pleased he was willing to say so.

"I don't know what to do anymore, and every time I try to give you what you say you need, it turns into another disaster."

He squatted down in front of her and claimed her hands in both of his. She noted how callused they were, the knuckles chafed, yet to her they were the most beautiful male hands she'd ever seen.

"You wanted romance, and I swear to you, Sherry, I've given it my best shot. If it's romantic to be nearly arrested for a woman, then I should get some kind of award, don't you think?"

She nodded.

"I don't blame you for my stumbling into a patch of poison ivy—that was my own fault. I wanted to impress you with the bluebonnets. I could have brought you a bouquet of carnations and that fancy grass that goes with them from the market. Les Gilles sells them for half price after seven, but I figured you'd think those wildflowers were a lot more romantic."

"I do. They're beautiful. Thank you."

"I've done every romantic thing I can think of for you. I don't know what else it is you want. I've sung to you, I've brought you candy—I know Heather's the one eating it, but I'll buy you another box."

"Don't worry about it."

"I am worried, not about the chocolates, but about everything else." He shook his head as if to clear the cobwebs. "I know you're concerned that Heather was the one who prompted the proposal, her wanting a baby brother and sister and all. In a way I suppose she did—in the beginning. I'm asking you to marry me again, only this time it's for me."

"Five minutes." Heather's voice thrilled from the other side of the door.

Cody briefly closed his eyes, stood and marched over to the door. "Heather, I asked for some time alone with Sherry, remember?"

"I'm just telling you you've used up ten of those minutes, and you only have five more. I can't be late, Dad, or Angela will be gone and my algebra book with her."

"I remember."

"Dad, you've wasted another whole minute of that time lecturing me."

Cody shook his head helplessly and returned to Sherry's side. "Now, where was I?"

"We were discussing your proposal."

"Right." He wiped his face as if that would help him say what he wanted to say. "I don't know what more it is you want from me. I've made a first-class fool of myself over you. I've done my damnedest to be the kind of man you want, but I can't be something when I don't have a clue what you're asking me to be. I don't know how to be romantic. All I know is how to be me. I'm wondering if that'll ever be good enough for you."

"Stop." She raised both hands. "Go back to what you were saying before Heather interrupted you."

He looked confused.

"You said you were asking me to marry you, not for Heather's sake, but for yourself."

"So?"

"So," she said, scooting forward in her chair, "are you trying to tell me you love me?"

He stopped his pacing and rubbed his hand along the back of his neck. "I'm not going to lie to you, Sherry—that would be too easy. I don't know if I love you, but I know there hasn't been a woman in the last decade who makes me feel the things you do. I've swallowed my pride for you, nearly been arrested for you. I'm suffering a bout of poison ivy because all I think about is you."

His words sounded like the lyrics of a love song. Sherry was thrilled.

"Dad!"

"All right, all right," Cody said impatiently. "I'm coming."

Sherry got to her feet, not wanting him to leave. "I'll be over at the ranch one afternoon this week," she volunteered hastily. "That'll give us both time to think about what we want."

Cody smiled and briefly touched her face. "I'll do what I can to keep Heather out of our hair."

"I heard that!"

Cody chuckled and, leaning forward, kissed Sherry gently on the lips. "Your kisses are sweeter than any chocolate-covered cherries."

"Hey, Dad, that was good," Heather announced on her way through the door. "I didn't prompt him, either," she said to Sherry.

CHAPTER NINE

"I HATE TO IMPOSE on you," Ellie said for the third time.

"You're not imposing," Sherry insisted also for the third time. "Christina Lynn and I will get along royally, and Philip won't even know you're gone." As if to confirm her words, Christina Lynn crawled into Sherry's lap and planted a wet kiss on her cheek. "Now go," Sherry said, tucking the toddler against her hip and escorting Ellie to the door. "Your husband wants to celebrate your anniversary."

"I can't believe he arranged all this without my knowing!"

Luke appeared then, dressed in a dark suit, his hair still damp beneath his hat. His arm went around Ellie's waist. "We haven't been out to dinner in months."

"I know, but . . ."

"Go and enjoy yourself," Sherry insisted. The more she got to know Luke and Ellie, the more she grew to enjoy them as a couple. Luke wasn't as easy to know as his wife, but Sherry was touched by the strength of his love for Ellie and his family. Luke had contacted her early Tuesday morning to ask if she'd mind sitting with the children Wednesday night while he surprised Ellie with dinner to celebrate their third wedding anniversary. Sherry had been honored that he'd want her. He then told her there wasn't anyone he'd trust more with his children.

Later, when she arrived at the ranch and Ellie was putting the finishing touches on her makeup, Luke had proudly shown Sherry the gold necklace he'd purchased for his wife. Sherry knew her friend would be moved to tears when she saw it and told him so. Luke had beamed with pleasure.

"If Philip should wake," Ellie said, "there's a bottle of formula in the refrigerator."

"Ellie," Luke said pointedly, edging her toward the door. "We have a dinner reservation for six."

"But—"

"Go on, Ellie," Sherry urged. "Everything will be fine."

"I know. It's just that I've never left Philip before, and it seems a bit soon to be cutting the apron strings."

Sherry laughed and bounced Christina Lynn on her hip. "We're going to have a nice quiet evening all by ourselves."

"You're sure..."

"*Go*," Sherry said again. She stood on the porch with Christina Lynn as Luke and Ellie drove off. The little girl waved madly.

For the first half hour, Christina Lynn was content to show Sherry her toys. She dragged them into the living room and proudly demonstrated how each one worked. Sherry oohed and ahhed at all the appropriate moments. When the toddler finished, Sherry helped her return the toys to the treasure chest that Luke had made for his daughter.

Having grown tired of her game, Christina Lynn lay down on the floor and started to fuss. "Mama!" she demanded as if realizing for the first time that her mother wasn't there.

"Mommy and Daddy have gone out to eat," Sherry explained patiently. Thinking Christina Lynn might be hungry, she heated her dinner and set the little girl in her high chair. But apparently Christina Lynn wasn't hungry, because the meal landed on the floor in record time.

"Mama!" Christina yelled, banging her little fists on the high-chair tray.

"Mommy's out with Daddy, sweetheart."

Christina Lynn's lower lip started to wobble.

"Don't cry, honey," Sherry pleaded but to no avail. Within seconds Christina Lynn was in full voice.

Sherry lifted her from the high chair and carried her into the living room. She sat in the rocker trying to soothe the child, but Christina Lynn only wept louder.

Inevitably her crying awoke Philip. With Christina Lynn gripping her leg for all she was worth, Sherry lifted the whimpering infant from his bassinet and changed his diaper. Lifting him over her shoulder, she gently patted his back, hoping to urge him back to sleep.

That, however, proved difficult, especially with Christina Lynn still at full throttle. The little girl was wrapped around Sherry's leg like a plaster and, both she and Philip were wailing loud enough to bring down the house. And this was how Sherry was when Cody found her.

She didn't hear Cody come in so was surprised to turn and find him standing in the hallway outside the children's bedroom, grinning hugely.

"Hi," he said. "Luke told me you were sitting with the kids tonight. It looks like you could use a little bit of help."

"Christina Lynn," Sherry said gratefully, "look— Uncle Cody's here."

Cody moved into the room and dislodged the toddler from Sherry's leg, lifting her into his arms. Christina Lynn buried her face in his shoulder and continued her tearful performance.

"What's wrong with Philip?" Cody asked over the din.

"I think he might be hungry. If you keep Christina Lynn occupied, I'll go heat his bottle."

They met in the living room, Sherry carrying the baby and the bottle. Cody was down on the floor, attempting to interest the toddler in a five-piece wood puzzle, but the little girl wanted none of it.

Philip apparently felt the same way about the bottle. "He's used to his mother breast-feeding him," Sherry said. "The nipple on the bottle is nothing like Ellie. Besides, I don't think he's all that hungry. If he was, he'd figure out this nipple business quick enough."

She returned the bottle to the kitchen and sat down in the chair with Philip, rocking him until his cries abated. Christina Lynn's wails turned to soft sobs as she buried her face in the sofa cushions.

"It looks like you've got your hands full."

Sherry gave a weary sigh. "Imagine Ellie handling them both, day in and day out. The woman's a marvel."

"So are you."

"Hardly." Sherry didn't mean to discount his compliment, but she was exhausted, and Luke and Ellie hadn't been gone more than a couple of hours. "I don't know how Ellie does it."

"Or Luke," Cody added. He slumped onto the end of the sofa and lifted an unresisting Christina Lynn into his arms. She cuddled against him, burying her face in his shirt.

At last silence reigned. "Come sit by me," Cody urged Sherry, stretching his arm along the back of the couch.

Sherry was almost afraid to move for fear Philip would awake, but her concern proved groundless. The infant didn't so much as sigh as she moved over to Cody's side. As soon as she was comfortable, Cody dropped his arm to her shoulder and pulled her closer. It was wonderful to be sitting this way with him, so warm and intimate.

"Peace at last," he whispered. "I'm wondering if I dare kiss you."

Sherry smiled softly. "You like to live dangerously, don't you?" She lifted her head and Cody's mouth brushed hers. Softly at first, moving back and forth several times, creating an exciting friction between them. Then he deepened the kiss, his lips urging hers apart until she was so involved in what was happening between them she nearly forgot Philip was in her arms.

She broke off the kiss and exhaled on a ragged sigh. "You're one powerful kisser."

"It isn't me, Sherry. It's us."

"Whomever or whatever, it's dangerous." She nestled her head against his shoulder. "I don't think we'd better do that again."

"Oh, I plan to do it again soon, and often."

"Cody," she said, lifting her head so their eyes could meet, "I'm not here to, uh, make out with you."

"Shh." He pressed his finger to her lips.

She pressed her head back against his shoulder. His arm was about her, anchoring her to him. She enjoyed the feeling of being linked to him, of being close, both physically and emotionally. It was what she'd sought from the beginning, this bonding, this intimacy.

She closed her eyes, savoring the warm, vital feel of him. Cody rubbed the underside of his jaw over the top of her head and she felt his breathing quicken. She straightened and read the hunger in his eyes, knowing it was a reflection of her own need. He lowered his mouth to hers, claiming her with a kiss that left her weak and clinging.

She was trembling inside and out. Neither of them spoke as they kissed again and again, each one more potent than the last. After many minutes, Sherry pulled back, almost gasping with pleasure and excitement.

"I can't believe we're doing this," she whispered. Each held a sleeping child in their arms. They were in their friends' home and could be interrupted at anytime.

"I can't believe it, either," Cody agreed. "Damn, but you're beautiful."

They didn't speak for a few minutes, just sat and savored the silence and each other.

"Sherry, listen—" Cody began.

He was interrupted by the shrill ringing of the telephone. Philip's piercing cry joined that of the phone. Christina Lynn awoke, too, and after taking one look at Cody and Sherry, burst into tears and cried out for her mom.

Cody got up to answer the phone. He was back on the couch in no time. He cast Sherry a frustrated look. "That was my daughter. She heard I was over here helping you baby-sit Christina Lynn and Philip, and she's madder than hops that I left her at home."

"It seems to me," Sherry said, patting Philip's back, "she got her revenge."

Cody grinned. "It was selfish of me not to bring her, but I wanted to be alone with you."

"We aren't exactly alone," she said. Her gaze moved to Luke and Ellie's children, who had miraculously calmed down again and seemed to be drifting off.

"True, but I was counting on them both being in bed asleep. Luke thought they would be and—"

"Luke," Sherry interrupted, pretending to be offended. "Do you mean to tell me this was all prearranged between you and Luke?"

"Well . . ."

"Did you?" Sherry could have sworn Cody was blushing.

"This all came about because of you and the fuss you made over wanting romance. Luke got a bit whimsical and thought he'd like to do something special for his and Ellie's anniversary. Then he worried that Ellie wouldn't want to leave the kids. It's hard to be romantic with a pair of kids around.''

Sherry looked at Christina Lynn and Philip and smiled. ''They didn't seem to deter us.''

''True, but we're the exception.'' After a pause he said, ''Put your head back on my shoulder.'' He looped his arm around her. ''It feels good to have you close.''

''It feels good to me, too.''

He kissed the crown of her head. Sherry closed her eyes, never dreaming she'd fall asleep, but she must have, because the next thing she heard was Luke and Ellie whispering.

She opened her eyes and her gaze met Ellie's smiling features. ''They were a handful, weren't they?''

''Not really,'' Sherry whispered.

''All four of you are worn to a frazzle. Even Cody's asleep.''

''I'm not now,'' he said, yawning loudly.

Ellie removed Philip from Sherry's arms, and Luke lifted his daughter from Cody's. The two disappeared down the hallway to the children's room, returning momentarily.

''How was your dinner?'' Sherry asked.

''Wonderful.'' Ellie's eyes were dreamy. She sat in the rocking chair while Luke moved into the kitchen. He reappeared a few moments later carrying a tray with four mugs of coffee.

''I can't remember an evening I've enjoyed more.'' Ellie's hand went to her throat and the single strand of gold that Luke had given her for their anniversary. "Thank you, Sherry."

"I'll be happy to watch the kids anytime."

"I don't mean for watching the kids—I mean, I certainly appreciate it, but there's more. Luke told me I should thank you because it was Cody talking to him about love and romance that made him realize he wanted our anniversary to be extra special this year."

Luke moved behind the rocking chair and leaned forward to kiss his wife's cheek.

"I think it's time we left," Cody suggested, "before this turns into something serious, or worse yet, something private."

"You could be right," Sherry agreed.

With eyes only for each other, Ellie and Luke didn't appear to notice they were leaving until Sherry was out the front door.

"Stick around, you two," Luke protested. "You haven't drunk your coffee."

"Another time," Cody answered, leading Sherry down the steps.

"Night," Sherry said to her friends.

"Night, and thanks again," Ellie said, standing in the doorway, her arm around her husband's waist, her head against his shoulder.

Cody escorted Sherry to her car, then hesitated before turning away. "I'll see you soon," he said frowning.

She was puzzled by the frown. She watched him as his gaze swung back to Luke in the doorway and then again to her. At last he sighed, rubbed his eyes and stepped away.

Sherry would gladly have given her first month's wages to know what Cody was thinking.

"DAD WAS FURIOUS with me," Heather announced when she stopped in at the clinic early the following afternoon. "He told me I had the worst sense of timing of anyone he's ever known. First the night he brought you the candy and flowers, and then when you were watching Christina Lynn and Philip.

"Slim got kicked by a horse once," the girl continued. "He was walking along behind this gelding, minding his own business, and the horse reared back and got him good. He was in a cast for six weeks. I reminded Dad of that, and he said my timing was even worse than Slim's."

"It's all right," Sherry assured her. "Your father and I'll get everything straightened out sooner or later." But Cody hadn't mentioned anything about them marrying lately, and Sherry was beginning to wonder.

"I'm not supposed to butt into your and Dad's business, and I don't mean to, but I really do hope you decide to marry us. I don't even care about the babies so much anymore. I really like you, Sherry, and it'd be so much fun if you were always around."

"I'd enjoy that, too."

"You would?" Sherry instantly brightened. "Can I tell Dad you said that, because I know he'd like to know and—"

"That might not be a good idea." Sherry removed her jacket and tossed it into the laundry container. She was finished for the day and eager to see Cody.

"I thought your friend Carrie was going to stop by with you," Sherry said.

"She couldn't. That's why I can't show you the way I want my hair cut."

"Oh, well. I'll see the magazine another time."

"Especially if you're going to be around awhile." Heather pressed her books against her chest and her eyes grew wistful. "I can hardly wait for you to move in with us."

"I didn't say I was moving in with you, Heather. Remember what Ellie told you at the picnic?"

Heather rolled her eyes exasperatedly as if reciting it for the hundredth time. "If I interfere with you and Dad, I could hurt more than help."

"You got it."

Before leaving the clinic, Sherry ran a brush through her hair and touched up her makeup. "You're sure Janey and your father are expecting me tonight?"

"Of course. Dad specifically suggested I stop by this evening and invite you out, but if you can't come, that's fine, too, because Slim's in town and he can take me home."

The phone rang just then, and Sherry let Mrs. Colson answer. The receptionist came back for Sherry.

"It's a nice-sounding young man asking for you."

This surprised Sherry. The only "nice sounding young man" who interested her was Cody Bailman, but Mrs. Colson would have recognized his voice.

She walked into her office and reached for the telephone. "This is Sherry Waterman."

"Sherry, it's Rowdy Cassidy. I know it's short notice, but I was wondering if you could fly to Houston for dinner tonight?"

"Fly to Houston? Tonight?"

"It's Norah's birthday, and I'd love to surprise her."

"But there isn't a plane for me to catch, and it'd take you hours for you to fly to Pepper to get me."

"I'm here now, at the airstrip outside of town."

"Here?" Norah's husband was full of surprises.

"Yeah, I flew into Abilene this morning and I got to thinking on my way home about bringing you back with me. I know it's a lot to ask on such short notice, but it'd give Norah such a boost. She loves Texas, but after your visit, she got real homesick. It'd mean a lot to her if you'd come and help her celebrate her birthday."

Sherry hesitated and looked at Heather, not wanting to disappoint Cody's daughter, either. "I need to be back by nine tomorrow morning."

"No problem. I can have one of my men fly you back tonight. What do you say?"

"Uh . . ." Sherry wished she had more time to think this over. "Sure," she said finally. "Why not?" Norah was her best friend, and she missed her, too.

They made the arrangements to meet, and Sherry hung up. "You heard?" she asked Heather.

Heather lowered her gaze dejectedly and nodded.

"It's for a surprise. Norah's the reason I moved to Texas, and she'd do it for me. Besides, you said Slim can take you back to the ranch."

"Yeah, I know."

"How about if you stop by after school tomorrow?" Sherry asked, hating to disappoint Heather. "It'd be even better, wouldn't it, because Carrie might be able to come."

Once more Heather nodded, but not with a lot of enthusiasm. "You're right. It's just that I was really looking forward to having you out at the ranch again. I think Dad was, too."

"There'll be lots of other times, I promise. You'll explain to your father, won't you?"

Heather nodded. Sherry dropped her off at the feed store where Slim's pickup was parked. She stayed long enough to be sure the older man was available to drive Heather back to the ranch.

From there she drove to the landing strip where Rowdy was waiting. How like a man to think of this at the last minute!

After greetings and hugs, Sherry boarded Rowdy's company jet and settled back in the cushioned seat.

"So how's Pepper been treating you?" Rowdy asked.

"Very well. I love Texas."

"Any progress with that cattleman?"

She smiled. "Some."

"Norah's going to be glad to hear that." He slapped his knee. "She's going to be very surprised to see you, but she's going to be even more surprised to see her father. He arrived earlier this afternoon. My driver picked him up at the airport and is going to give him a quick tour of Houston and Galveston Island. If everything goes according to schedule, we should arrive at the house at about the same time."

"You thought all this up on your own?"

"Yep." He looked extremely proud of himself. "I talked to Norah's father a couple of months back about flying out, but as I explained, having you join us was a spur-of-the-moment idea. Norah's going to be thrilled. I love surprising her."

To say that Norah was surprised was putting it mildly. As Rowdy predicted, David Bloomfield arrived within minutes of her and Rowdy. They'd waited in the driveway for him, and the three of them walked into the house together.

Rowdy stood in the entryway and, his eyes twinkling, called, "Norah, I'm home!"

Norah appeared and Rowdy threw open his arms. "Happy birthday!" he shouted, and stepped aside to reveal David Bloomfield and Sherry, standing directly behind him.

"Daddy!" Norah cried, enthusiastically hugging her father first. "Sherry!" Norah wrapped her arms around her and squeezed tight, her eyes bright with tears.

"You thought I forgot your birthday, didn't you?" Rowdy crowed.

Norah wiped the moisture from her face and nodded. "I really did. I had the most miserable day. The kids were both fussy, and I felt like I'd moved to the ends of the earth and everyone had forgotten me."

"This is a long way from Orchard Valley," her father said, putting his arm around his youngest daughter's shoulder, "but it isn't the end of the world—although I think I might be able to see it from here."

Norah chuckled. "Oh, Dad, that's an old joke."

"You laughed, didn't you?"

"Come on in and make yourselves comfortable," Rowdy invited, ushering them into the living room. "I certainly hope you didn't go to any trouble for dinner," he said to his wife.

"No. I was feeling sorry for myself and thought we'd order pizza. It's been that kind of day."

"Good—" Rowdy paused and looked at his watch. "—because the caterer should arrive in about ten minutes."

Norah was floored. "Is there anything else I should know about?"

"This?" He removed a little velvet box from his pocket, then put it back. "Think I'll save that for later when we're alone."

David laughed and looked around. "Now, where are those precious grandchildren of mine?"

"Sleeping. They're both exhausted. But if you promise to be quiet, I'll take you upstairs for a peek. How long are you staying? A week, I hope."

David and Sherry followed Norah upstairs and tip-toed into the children's rooms. Sherry was fond of David Bloomfield and loved watching his reaction as he looked at his grandchildren. Sherry remembered several years back when David had suffered a heart attack and almost died. His recovery had been nothing short of miraculous.

By the time they came back downstairs, the caterer had arrived and the table was set for an elegant dinner. The candles were lit and the appetizers served.

"Rowdy did this once before," Norah said, reaching for her husband's hand. Rowdy brought her fingers to his mouth and brushed his lips over them. "He wanted something then. Dinner was all part of a bribe to get me to leave Orchard Valley and be his private nurse."

Rowdy laughed. "It didn't work, either. Norah didn't believe I loved her, and I can't say I blame her, since I didn't know it myself. All I knew was that I couldn't imagine my life without her. You led me on quite a merry chase—but I wouldn't have had it any differently."

"Are you looking to bribe my daughter this time?" David asked.

Rowdy shook his head. "Nope. I have everything I need."

The shrimp appetizer was followed by a heart-of-palm salad. Norah turned to Sherry. "How's everything going between you and Cody?"

Sherry shrugged, unsure how much she should say. "Better."

"I have to tell you, I got a kick out of your last letter. He actually proposed to you by saying he wanted to cut to the chase?"

"Sounds like a man who knows what he wants," Rowdy commented.

"Cody's come a long way since then. He's trying hard to understand what I want, but I don't think he's quite figured it yet." She lowered her gaze and sighed. "Currently he's suffering from the effects of poison ivy. He ran into a patch of it while picking wildflowers for me."

"Well, he's certainly trying hard."

"I wish now I'd been more specific," Sherry said, smoothing her napkin. "I love Cody and I want romance, yes, but more than that, I want him to share himself with me, his thoughts and ideas, his dreams for the future. What troubles him most is the fear that if he loves me he'll lose his identity. He says he isn't willing to let any woman put a collar around his neck."

"Sounds reasonable." David said.

"He's really very dear." Sherry wanted to be sure everyone understood her feelings.

"You love him?"

Sherry nodded. "I did almost from the first."

"Let me talk to him," Rowdy offered, "man to man."

"It wouldn't do any good," Sherry said, trying to sound upbeat. "His best friend, who's happily married, tried, and Cody just thinks Luke's lost his marbles."

"He'll feel differently once he's married himself."

"Didn't you tell me Cody has a twelve-year-old daughter?" Norah asked.

Sherry nodded. "I don't know a lot about his marriage, just enough to know they were both pretty immature. His wife was killed in an automobile accident years ago."

"And he's never thought about marrying again until now?" David inquired.

"Heather had a lot to do with his proposing to me, but—" She stopped, remembering how Cody had told her that the first time he'd asked her to marry him it'd been for Heather's sake, but now it was for his own. "With time, I believe he'll understand it isn't wildflowers that interest me, or serenading me in the dead of night—it's trusting and sharing. It's a sense of belonging to each other."

"It's sitting up together with a sick baby," Norah added.

"And loving your partner enough to allow them to be themselves," Rowdy continued.

"And looking back over the years you were to-gether and knowing they were the best ones of your life," David added thoughtfully.

Sherry hoped that in time Cody would understand all this. His mother had asked her to be patient, and Ellie had given her the same advice. It was difficult at times, but she held on to the promise of everything eventually working together.

Sherry left early the following morning. Norah walked out to the car with her, dressed in her robe, her eyes sleepy. "I wish you could stay longer."

"I do, too."

"If you ever want to get away for a weekend, let me know, and I'll have Rowdy send a plane for you."

"I will. I promise."

The flight back to Pepper seemed to take only half the time the ride into Houston had. Her car was waiting for her when she arrived at the airfield. She glanced at her watch, pleased to see she had plenty of time before she was on duty at the clinic.

Driving down Main Street, Sherry was struck once more by the welcome she felt in Pepper. It was as if she belonged here and always would. The sight of Cody's pickup parked in front of the clinic came as a surprise. She pulled around to the back of the building to her appointed slot and came in the back door.

Cody wasn't anywhere in sight. "Mrs. Colson," she asked, walking out front. "Have you seen Cody?"

"No, I was wondering that myself. His truck's here, but he doesn't seem to be around."

Stepping onto the porch, Sherry glanced around. A movement, ever so slight, from Cody's truck caught her eye. She moved down the walkway to discover Cody fast asleep in the cab.

"Cody," she called softly through the open window, not wanting to startle him. "What are you doing here?"

"Sherry?" He bolted upright, banging his head on the steering wheel. "Damn!" he muttered, rubbing the injured spot. He opened the door and nearly fell onto the street in his eagerness.

"Have you been drinking?" she demanded.

"No," he returned angrily. "Where the hell have you been all night?"

"With my friend in Houston," she told him, "although where I was or who I was with isn't any of your business."

"Some hotshot with a Learjet, from what I heard."

"Yes. As I understand it, Rowdy's something of a legend."

"I see." Cody slammed his hat onto his head. "What are you trying to do? Make me jealous?"

"Oh, for crying out loud, that's the stupidest thing you've ever said to me, Cody Bailman, and you've said some real doozies. Rowdy's married."

"So you're flying off with married men now?"

"Rowdy's married to my best friend, Norah. It was her birthday yesterday, and on his way home from Abilene, he decided to surprise Norah by bringing me home with him."

Cody frowned as if he didn't believe her. "That's not the story Heather gave me. She said I had to do something quick, because you were seeing another man." Cody paced the sidewalk in front of her like a caged bear. "This is it, Sherry. I'm not willing to play any more games with you. I've done everything I know to prove to you I'm sincere, so if you want to run off with a married man at this point—"

"I didn't run off with a married man!" she said hotly. "For you to even suggest I did is ridiculous."

"I spent the entire night sleeping in my pickup, waiting for you to get back, so if I happen to be a bit short-tempered, you can figure out why."

"Then maybe you should just go home and think this through before you start throwing accusations at me."

"Maybe I should," he growled.

Sherry was mortified to glance around and notice they had an audience. Mrs. Colson was standing on the front porch enthralled with their conversation. The woman across the street who'd been watering her roses had long since lost interest in them and was inadvertently hosing down the sidewalk. Another couple rocking on their porch seemed to be enjoying the show, as well.

"I'm serious, Sherry. This is the last time I'm going to ask." Cody jerked open the truck door and leapt inside. "Are you going to marry me or not, because I've had it."

"That proposal's about as romantic as the first."

"You know what I think of romance." He started the engine and ground the gears.

He'd pulled away from the curb when she slammed her foot down on the pavement. "Yes, you idiot!" she screamed after him. "I'll marry you!"

CHAPTER TEN

"I DON'T THINK he heard you, dear," the lady watering the roses called, looking concerned.

"I don't think he did, either," the older man on the porch agreed, standing up and walking to his gate to get a better look at Sherry.

"Cody would never have driven away," Mrs. Colson said. "That dear man's beside himself for want of you. Cody may be stubborn, but he isn't stupid. Mark my words, he'll come to his senses soon."

Sherry wasn't sure she wanted him to. The man was too infuriating, suggesting she was seeing a married man behind his back.

"Do you want me to phone Cody for you, dear, and explain?" Mrs. Colson suggested as Sherry marched up the stairs and in the front doorway.

Sherry turned and glared angrily at the receptionist.

"It was only a suggestion." Mrs. Colson muttered.

"I prefer to do my own talking."

"Of course," Mrs. Colson said pleasantly, clearly not offended by the reprimand. "I'm positive everything will work out between you and Cody. Don't give a moment's heed to what he said earlier. Everyone knows he can be as stubborn as a mule."

"I'm not the least bit positive about anything having to do with that man," Sherry returned. Cody had been telling her for weeks that this was her last opportunity to marry him, and he wasn't going to ask her again.

A half hour later, when Sherry came out of her office reading a file Doc Lindsey had left for her to review, she heard Mrs. Colson speaking softly into the telephone.

"I swear you've never seen anyone so angry in all your life as Cody Bailman was this morning," she said. "He left half his tire on the street peeling out of here the way he did, and all because he's so crazy about—"

"Mrs. Colson," Sherry said.

The receptionist placed her hand over the receiver and barely glanced upward. "I'll be with you in just a minute." She put the receiver to her ear once more and continued, "And dear, dear Sherry, why she's so overwrought that she can hardly—"

Mrs. Colson froze, swallowed once, tightly, and then looked at Sherry. "Is there anything I can do for you?" she managed, her face flushing crimson.

"Yes," Sherry said. "You can kindly stop gossiping about me."

"Oh, dear, I was afraid of that. You've got the wrong impression. I never gossip—ask anyone. I have been known to pass on information, but I don't consider that gossiping." Abruptly she replaced the receiver.

Sherry glanced at the phone, wondering what the person on the other end was thinking.

"I was only trying to help," Mrs. Colson insisted. "Donna Jo's known Cody all his life and—"

"You were speaking to Donna Jo?" It amazed Sherry that anyone got any work done in this town.

"Why, yes. Donna Jo's friends with Cody's mother same as I am. She has a vested interest in what happens between you two. So do Mayor Bowie and the sheriff, and we both know those two spend a lot of time over there at the Yellow Rose."

"What's my schedule like this morning?" Sherry asked wearily.

Mrs. Colson flipped through the pages of the appointment book. "Mrs. O'Leary's due at ten, but she's been coming to see Doc for the past three years for the same thing."

"What's her problem?"

Mrs. Colson sighed heavily. "Mrs. O'Leary's over seventy and, well, she wants a nose job. She's convinced she lost Earl Burrows because her nose was too big, and that was more'n fifty years ago."

"Did she ever marry?"

"Oh, yes. She married Larry O'Leary, but I don't think it was a happy union, although she bore him eight sons. Doc says it's the most ridiculous thing he's ever heard of, a woman getting her nose done when she's seventy. When she comes in, he asks her to think about it for another six months. She's been coming back faithfully every six months for three years."

"If she sees me, I'll give her a referral. If she's that set on a new nose, then she should have it."

"I told Doris you'd feel that way—that's why I set the appointment up with you," Mrs. Colson said, looked pleased with herself. "If you want, I can save

Doris the trouble of coming in and give her the name of the referral.''

"All right. I'll make a few calls and be back to you in a couple of minutes. Am I scheduled to see anyone else?''

"Not until this afternoon." The receptionist looked almost gleeful with the news. "You're free to go for a long drive, if you like." She looked both ways, then added, "No one would blame you for slipping out for a few hours...."

Sherry wasn't sure if she was slipping out or flipping out. She made a couple of calls, gave the names of three plastic surgeons for Mrs. Colson to pass on to her first patient of the day and then reached for her purse.

She was halfway to the door when it burst open and Donna Jo rushed in. "I'm so glad I caught you!" she said excitedly. "You poor, poor girl," she said with liquid eyes, "you must be near crazy with worry."

"Worry?"

"About losing Cody. Now, you listen here, I've got some womanly advice for you." She paused, inhaled deeply and pressed her hand over her generous bosom. "Sherry Waterman, fight for your man. You love him—folks in town have known that for weeks—and we're willing to forgive you for leaving in that fancy jet with that handsome cowboy. By the way, who *was* that?"

"Rowdy Cassidy, and before you say another word, I didn't leave with him the way you're suggesting."

"We know that, dear."

"Rowdy Cassidy?" Martha Colson whispered, and nodded when Donna Jo's eyes questioned her. "Not *the* Rowdy Cassidy?"

"That's who she said," Donna Jo muttered irritably. "Now let her talk."

"There's nothing more to say." Sherry didn't want to spend what time she had talking about her excursion of the night before, although both women were eager for details. "I'm going to do as you suggest and take a long drive this morning."

"Now you be sure and stop in at the café and let me know what happens once you're through talking to Cody," Donna Jo instructed.

"Who said I was going to talk to Cody?"

"You *are* going to him, aren't you?" Donna Jo said. "You must. That poor dear is all thumbs when it comes to dealing with love and romance. Personally, I thought you did a smart thing, asking for a little romance first, but everyone agrees that the time's come for you to put Cody out of his misery."

"He's suffered enough," Mrs. Colson added.

"Who would have believed Cody Bailman would be like this with a woman. I will say it took a mighty special one," Donna Jo concluded, winking at Sherry.

With half the town awaiting the outcome, Sherry hopped in her car and drove out to Cody's ranch. Odds were he was working out on the range, so she wasn't sure what good her visit would do. Nevertheless, she had to try.

She saw Cody almost immediately. He was working with a gelding in the corral when she arrived, leading him by the reins around the enclosed area.

Climbing out of her car, Sherry walked over to the fence and stood for several moments, waiting for Cody to notice her. He seemed preoccupied with the task at hand, putting the gelding through his paces. Sherry was certain he knew she was there, and she was willing to be ignored for only so long.

Five of the slowest minutes of her life passed before she stepped onto the bottom rung of the fence and braced her arms on the top one.

"Cody!"

He turned to face her, his eyes blank.

This was much harder than Sherry had expected. On the drive out to his ranch, she'd envisioned Cody's eyes lighting up with pleasure at the sight of her. She'd imagined him hugging her, lifting her from the ground and swinging her around, his eyes filled with love and promises.

"Yes?" he said at last.

"When you drove away this morning, I . . . I didn't think you heard me," she offered weakly.

Cody led the gelding over to one of his hired hands, removed his hat long enough to wipe his brow with his forearm and then strolled toward her as if he had all the time in the world.

Sherry found it impossible to read him. He revealed no emotion. He might as well have been an android.

"I . . . don't think you're ready to talk yet," Sherry said.

"You were the one who suggested I go home."

"I know, but I was hoping you'd have thought things out by now and realized I would never date my best friend's husband." Or anyone else when she was so desperately in love with Cody. It seemed as if their time together with Christina Lynn and Philip had been forgotten.

"It was Rowdy Cassidy you left with, wasn't it?"

Sherry nodded.

"I must say you certainly have friends in high places."

"It's Norah I know, not Rowdy."

"Yet you left on a moment's notice with a man who is virtually a stranger."

Sherry closed her eyes and prayed for patience. "Would you stop being so damn stubborn! If you honestly believe I'm the type of woman to run around with a married man, then you don't know me at all."

"*My* stubbornness!" he exploded. "Do you realize what I've gone through because of you? I've been the brunt of jokes for weeks. My reputation with the other ranchers is in shambles, and furthermore I'm still scratching." He removed his glove, rolled up a sleeve and scraped his fingernails across his forearm. "I've done everything I know to earn your love, and I'm finished. I've gone as far as I'm willing to go."

"That's the problem. You want my love, but you aren't willing to give me yours. It wasn't romance I was looking for, Cody, it was love. I wanted you to care enough for me that you'd be willing to do whatever it took to win my heart." She pressed her hand over her heart and felt it beating hard and strong against her palm. "You never understood that. From the first you've been looking for the shortcut, because you didn't want to be bothered. No woman wants to be considered an annoyance."

"So that's what you think of me."

"What am I supposed to think with you saying the things you do?"

"That's just fine and dandy."

He turned away from her as if this was the end of their conversation, as if everything that needed to be said had been said. Sherry knew a brush-off when she saw one. Whatever more she might say would fall on deaf ears.

She walked over to her car, climbed in and started the engine. She'd shifted into gear and started to drive away when she changed her mind. Easing the car into reverse, she pulled alongside the corral fence and stuck her head out the open window intending to shout at him, but in her frustration, no words came.

She pulled out of the yard hell-bent for leather. It had been a mistake to try to reason with Cody. Her better judgment insisted she wait several days and let matters cool before she attempted to reopen communication. She should have listened to her own heart instead of Mrs. Colson's and Donna Jo's eagerly offered advice.

Sherry wasn't sure what caused her to look in her rearview mirror, but when she did, her breath jammed in her throat. Cody was riding bareback after her, atop the gelding he'd been working with moments earlier. The horse was in full gallop, and Cody looked as if he were riding for the pony express, whipping the reins across the animal's neck. Sherry was astonished that he managed to stay astride.

She eased to a stop, and so did the gelding. Cody leapt off his back and jerked open her car door.

"Are you going to marry me or not?" he demanded. He was panting harshly.

Sherry eyed him calmly. "Do you love me?"

"After everything I've been through, how can you ask me a question like that!" he snapped. "Yes, I love you. You've been carrying my heart with you for weeks. What does it take to convince you I'm sincere? Blood?"

"No," she whispered, biting her trembling lower lip.

"I love you, Sherry Waterman," he said. "Would you do me the supreme honor of being my wife?"

She nodded through her tears.

"Hot damn!" he shouted, then hauled Sherry into his arms so fast her breath fled her lungs. His mouth was over hers as if he were starving and she were bread hot from the oven.

His kiss left her weak. "Cody..." she said, breaking away from him. "You maniac. You chased after my car on a horse just the way Luke came after Ellie, and you always said that was such a stupid thing to do."

He opened his mouth as though to deny it, then realized it was true. He blinked several times, then smiled sheepishly. "So I did. Guess this is what love does to a man."

"Do you really love me?"

"Love you?" he cried. "Yes, Sherry, I love you."

"But you—"

"Don't even say it. Damn, but you led me on a crazy chase, woman." He kissed her again, this one far less urgent, more...loving. After a few minutes he released her and said, "Let's go."

"Where?" she asked.

"Where else? A preacher. You're not going to get the opportunity to change your mind."

She looped her arms around his neck again. "I'm not going to, not ever." It was Sherry who did the kissing this time, and when they finished, Cody was leaning against the side of her car. His eyes were closed and his breaths were deep, heavy. Then he reached for her again and swung her off the ground.

"Put me down," Sherry said, "I'm too heavy."

"No, you're not," Cody declared. "I'm calling the preacher right now and we'll get the license this afternoon."

"Cody," she said, "Put me down!"

He finally did so, then eyed her firmly. "I've waited ten long years for you, sweetheart, and I'm not putting this wedding off for another moment. If you want one of those big fancy weddings, then..." he paused as if he wasn't sure what he'd do.

"A small ceremony is fine." She grinned.

"With a reception big enough to fill the state of Texas, if that's what you want."

"I want my family here."

"I'll have airplane tickets waiting for them by noon."

"Cody, are we crazy?"

"Yes, for one another, and that's just the way it's supposed to be. Luke told me that, and I didn't understand it until I met you. By heaven, woman, what took you so damn long?"

She stared at him and felt the laughter bubble up inside her. Wrapping her arms around his neck, she kissed him soundly. "For the life of me I don't know."

SHERRY RETURNED to the office sometime later to find both Mrs. Colson and Donna Jo standing on the porch, eagerly waiting for her.

Sherry greeted them warmly, as she strolled past.

"How'd it go with Cody?" Donna Jo asked urgently. The pair followed her into the clinic.

"Everything went fine," Sherry said, enjoying keeping them guessing.

"Fine?" Mrs. Colson repeated. She looked at Donna Jo. "What does 'fine' tell us?"

"Nothing," the waitress responded. "I learned a long time ago not to listen to the words, but to study the expression. 'Fine' to me, the way Sherry just said it, says there's going to be a wedding in Pepper real soon."

"Isn't the lunch crowd at the café by now?" Sherry asked.

"Ellen can handle it," Donna Jo said, sitting in the closest chair.

"She's not wearing a diamond," Martha Colson said.

"No diamond?" Donna Jo looked incredulous. "I was sure you'd come back sporting the biggest rock this side of Mexico."

"You mean one this size?" Sherry dug into her purse and pulled out the one Cody had given her. She slipped it in her finger feeling heady with joy and excitement. Mrs. Colson and Donna Jo screamed with delight and Sherry hugged them both.

"When's the wedding?"

"Soon, just the way you said," Sherry told them, her heart warming. They'd contacted Sherry's family and made what arrangements they could over the phone. Afterward, Cody had given her the ring, one he'd been patiently carrying with him for weeks.

Sherry wasn't able to explain more. The front door opened, and Heather let out a cry and vaulted into her arms.

"Who told you?" Sherry asked when she got her breath. Cody had planned to pick his daughter up after school and bring her over to the clinic so they could tell her together.

"Dad," Heather explained. "He came by the school. Men are so funny—they can't keep a secret at all."

Cody walked into the clinic, looking sheepish. "You don't mind, do you?"

"Of course not." Sherry hugged her soon-to-be-daughter.

"Hey, I need a hug, too," Cody said, wrapping his arms around Sherry and holding her against him. With her hands at either side of his face, she pulled.

"Now that's romantic," Mrs. Colson sighed.

"I could just cry," Sherry heard Donna Jo say.

"How soon do you think it'll be before Sherry has a baby?" Heather whispered.

"A year," Mrs. Colson suggested.

"Give them that at least that long," Donna Jo agreed.

"A year," Cody said, lifting his head and casting a weary eye toward his audience. He smiled down at Sherry and winked. "I don't think it'll take nearly that long."

Let

HARLEQUIN ROMANCE®

take you

BACK TO THE RANCH

Come to Shadow Mountain Ranch, near Jessup, California!

Meet Franzi DeLisle, who raises mules and distrusts lawmen.
And meet Levi Hunter, traditionalist, horse lover...
and U.S. Marshal.

Read STUBBORN AS A MULE
by Roz Denny, the August Back to the Ranch title!
Available in August wherever Harlequin books are sold.

RANCH3

Take 4 bestselling love stories FREE

Plus get a FREE surprise gift!

Special Limited-time Offer

Mail to Harlequin Reader Service®

3010 Walden Avenue
P.O. Box 1867
Buffalo, N.Y. 14269-1867

YES! Please send me 4 free Harlequin Romance® novels and my free surprise gift. Then send me 6 brand-new novels every month, which I will receive months before they appear in bookstores. Bill me at the low price of $2.24 each plus 25¢ delivery and applicable sales tax if any*. That's the complete price and—compared to the cover prices of $2.99 each—quite a bargain! I understand that accepting the books and gift places me under no obligation ever to buy any books. I can always return a shipment and cancel at any time. Even if I never buy another book from Harlequin, the 4 free books and the surprise gift are mine to keep forever.

116 BPA AJJD

Name	(PLEASE PRINT)	
Address	Apt. No.	
City	State	Zip

This offer is limited to one order per household and not valid to present Harlequin Romance® subscribers.
*Terms and prices are subject to change without notice. Sales tax applicable in N.Y.

UROM-93R

©1990 Harlequin Enterprises Limited

Harlequin Romance invites you...

BACK TO THE

As you enjoy your Harlequin Romance® BACK TO THE RANCH stories each month, you can collect four proofs of purchase to redeem for an attractive gold-toned charm bracelet complete with five Western-themed charms. The bracelet will make a unique addition to your jewelry collection or a distinctive gift for that special someone.

One proof of purchase can be found in the back pages of each BACK TO THE RANCH title...one every month until May 1994.

To receive your gift, please fill out the information below and mail four (4) original proof-of-purchase coupons from any Harlequin Romance **BACK TO THE RANCH** title plus $2.50 for postage and handling (check or money order—do not send cash), payable to Harlequin Books, to: **IN THE U.S.:** P.O. Box 9057, Buffalo, NY, 14269-9057; **IN CANADA:** P.O. Box 622, Fort Erie, Ontario, L2A 5X3.

Requests must be received by June 30, 1994.

Please allow 4-6 weeks after receipt of order for delivery.

BACK TO THE

NAME: _____

ADDRESS: _____

_____

CITY: _____

STATE/PROVINCE: _____

ZIP/POSTAL CODE: _____

ONE PROOF OF PURCHASE   089 KAX

089 KAX